D1564788

GRAVEYARD WORKING

OTHER WORKS BY GERALD DUFF

INDIAN GIVER, Bloomington, Indiana: University of Indiana Press, 1983. (Novel)

WILLIAM COBBETT AND THE POLITICS OF EARTH, Salzburg, Austria: University of Salzburg Press, 1972. Reprinted: Longman Group, London, 1986.

LETTERS OF WILLIAM COBBETT, Salzburg, Austria: University of Salzburg Press, 1972. Reprinted: Longman Group, London, 1986.

A CEREMONY OF LIGHT, Sussex, England: Interim Press, 1976. (Collection of poems)

CALLING COLLECT, University Presses of Florida, 1982. (Collection of poems)

Graveyard Working

a novel by

Gerald Duff

BASKERVILLE
PUBLISHERS, INC.
DALLAS • NEW YORK • DUBLIN

BASKERVILLE Publishers, Inc.
7616 LBJ Freeway, Suite 220, Dallas TX 75251-1008

Parts of two sections of this book have been previously published in different form. A portion was published as "Fire Ants" in *Ploughshares Magazine* in 1985. Another portion was published as "The Motion of the Animals" in *Missouri Review* in 1988.

Library of Congress Cataloging-in-Publication Data

Duff, Gerald.
  Graveyard working : a novel / by Gerald Duff.
      p.   cm.
    ISBN: 1-880909-15-4 (lib. bdg.) : $18.00
    1. Aged women--Family--Texas--Fiction. 2. Sisters--Texas--
Fiction   I. Title
PS3554.U3177G7 1994
813'.54--dc20   93-43974
                                                  CIP

For Patricia Stephens
I would name a town in Texas for you.

*Commonly in the rural south, one day each year
was designated for family and friends to gather for
the purpose of cleaning and scraping the grave sites.
Food is brought and served from long tables near the
cemetery. The association of eating and the dead can
perhaps be traced to Old World pagan ceremonial
cannibalism, involving the eating of dead relatives.*

*from "The Material Culture of the
Traditional East Texas Graveyard"
by Anita Pitchford*

I

Drought

The mark was still there. When MayBelle turned over to check it, as she had done every morning for the last thirty-two years, she could see it, sure enough, high up on the left door-facing. It was almost all filled in with paint now, chipped away in layers of white, gray, blue green, a yellow the color of squash that Myrtle had had a man swab all over every wall in the house twenty or so years ago, but still visible. She didn't need glasses to see it.

MayBelle closed her eyes and opened them again so she could see the scarred place as if for the first time that morning. Outside the window a mockingbird, the state bird of Texas, began imitating a jay and switched in the middle of its cry to the last two notes of a quail's call. It then repeated the whole thing over again in reverse order, trailing off on the last note as if it was too hot to carry on.

MayBelle lifted the sheet and fanned herself a time or two but didn't feel any cooler. Here it was the first week in August, the week of Big Caney, and it hadn't rained in sixty-three days. The mockingbird by the window made one more squawk and then gave it up. Maybelle could see the limb he'd been sitting on rub up against the screen after he'd flapped off, looking for shade.

"Hot, hot," Myrtle said from the room down the hall, loud enough to be heard through the two closed doors. MayBelle closed her eyes and stayed quiet, flapping the sheet one more time to get a little air going and moved her legs to a cooler spot on the bed.

"Oh, MayBelle, I said hot, hot," said Myrtle in a stronger voice, getting more throat into it this time.

She's probably setting up to holler better, Maybelle thought, and flopped over under the sheet to answer. "You say *pot, pot*? What pot are talking about? You mean that old blue enamel thing?"

"No, I didn't say pot. What are you saying about a blue enamel pot? I said it was hot. Hot as the hinges of you know where, and him coming today. Driving in all this heat clean from Corpus Christi."

The door banged open, and Myrtle came shuffling down the hall toward MayBelle's room, leaning with first one hand, then the other against the walls as she worked her way on down the carpet of the corridor. She came into the room breathing through her mouth in loud puffs and swatting at the strands of hair that had worked their way loose from the net around her head sometime in the night.

"Blessed Savior," she said, standing at the end of MayBelle's bed and holding on to the footboard, "Sweet Jesus, I forgot my teeth."

4

"Say you forgot your belief?" MayBelle fanned the sheet and looked for a new cool spot with her right leg.

"Teeth," said Myrtle, baring orange gums and pointing into her mouth with her free hand. Her housecoat had fallen open, and MayBelle looked off to avoid seeing the points her nipples made under the flannel nightgown. She never could stand looking at her sister's private parts, not when they were girls sleeping in the same bed in Papa's house and not since. Her parts were always overdeveloped and Myrtle and everybody else had always paid so much attention to them that MayBelle would just as soon pretend they weren't even there. Better if they never had been. MayBelle turned over in bed with her back toward Myrtle and looked through the window toward the little patch of woods where the mockingbird had flown. The leaves drooped in the heat, and not a breath of air was moving.

"Coming from Corpus in this kind of weather," said Myrtle. "I hope B.J. don't get too hot driving. He'll be so tired. He preached two services yesterday. Probably did some baptizing too, I reckon." She leaned against the footboard until it creaked.

"That car's air-conditioned, ain't it? B.J. never did work himself until he was sick neither. I don't remember it if he did." Somewhere far off MayBelle heard a tractor crank up.

"Am I gonna have to beg you to get me my teeth out of that glass of water or am I supposed to crawl back down that hall myself?" Myrtle tottered, pulled at the footboard, and put a hand across her eyes. "Big Caney this coming Sunday," she said in a weak voice, "another year gone."

"I'll get them again," MayBelle said and threw back the sheet. "Go on in the kitchen. There ain't another speck of coolness in this bed."

When she walked into the kitchen, the glassful of teeth held off to the one side where she couldn't see them grinning at her, MayBelle found her sister leaning against the back door jamb talking through the screen to somebody. It was Cora, just about

5

the last old-timey colored woman left in Annette. She had walked up across the back pasture from where she lived in one of the collection of rundown unpainted shacks still known in town as the quarter. She stood now with one foot up on the lowest step to the back porch, balancing herself by swinging a silver-colored lard bucket out to one side. She was wearing a man's army overcoat in spite of this heat and had her head tied in a scarf that had the map of some state painted on it. Which one MayBelle couldn't tell, but it looked like one of the square-shaped ones up north.

"Didn't them guard dogs bark when you walked up, Cora?" Myrtle was asking her.

The old woman swung around to look at the pen behind her and studied for a minute. The three Dobermans and the five German shepherds were all lined up at the fence, tails wagging and tongues hanging out, none of them making a sound except for one of the Dobermans which made a yawning noise as the women watched.

"Nome," said Cora. "Now, that littlest one, he noticed me when I come up. How I know is he come running up to the gate yonder wanting me to let him out I guess. He the pretty one. He just wag his tail and smile."

"Did you hear that, MayBelle?" Myrtle said over her shoulder. "Not a one of B.J.'s guard dogs made a peep at that old colored woman."

She swung back away from the screen door and stuck out her hand toward the glass of teeth. "I just don't know what he's going to say. You haven't been doing a thing to make them mean. Lord knows I'm not able to."

"What you want this hot morning, Cora?" asked MayBelle, stepping around Myrtle and pushing open the screen. "Ain't you scared of meeting snakes coming through them high weeds in that pasture land?"

"Nome, Miss MayBelle," Cora said and waved her bucket

at the guard dogs before she turned back to the porch. A couple of the shepherds flopped down into the dust of the pen as though she had just given them a signal. "I ain't studying no snakes these days. It's done and got too hot for the boosters to mess with a old woman like I is. I stays away from them fire ants, though."

Behind her MayBelle could hear Myrtle rummaging through the pots and pans in the kitchen, and off across the pasture she could see a thin plume of yellowish smoke rising straight up in the dead air from one of the cabins in the quarter. It looked like a school picture that one of B.J.'s and Peachie's kids might have drawn with crayolas. But it didn't look finished, and MayBelle couldn't tell exactly which cabin chimney the smoke was coming from.

"Did you need a fire in the house this morning, Cora?" She pointed over the old woman's head toward the children's picture across the pasture.

"Nope, I didn't build no fire up today. I sleeped in my coat and I dranked my coffee cold this morning." Cora turned and leaned toward the horizon, her hand up to shade her eyes while she looked.

"That air smoke old Sully's fire."

"I thought you was the last one living in the quarter nowadays, Cora."

"I wish I was. That old Sully still yonder." The black woman turned back to the porch and shook her lard bucket. "He still bothering too."

"What you mean bothering?"

"Don't get her started now, MayBelle," Myrtle called through the screen. "You know what nastiness she wants to talk about."

MayBelle moved a step further out on the porch, and Cora pitched her voice lower. "What I mean about old Sully, he still trying to midnight crawl. He a creeper still." Cora shifted her

7

lard bucket and climbed up a step higher. "He come a scratching on my screen last night. Onliest thing awake be him and the hoot owls." The old black woman's voice began slipping into a sing-song and she began to sway back and forth as she talked. MayBelle made another little advance toward her and pulled her coat a shade tighter. The smoke from the cabin across the pasture hung in the sky like a ribbon.

"He wake me up a scratching, talking low, trying to sweet his way in the house."

"Ain't he too old for that kind of stuff?" MayBelle said, trying to look into the old woman's cloudy eyes and having a hard time getting past a kind of film that seemed to lay on their surface like the skin on milk being heated.

"He say not. He say it's still good times. It's fire in the stove yet he say."

"What did you say to him? Did you let him keep on talking?"

"Can't stop him from talking. He a talker." The old woman swayed a couple of beats more as she paused. "And a creeper," she added after a minute.

"Did you let him keep on?"

"He got to keep on. Ain't no quit in him. He bound to keep on."

"MayBelle," Myrtle called from the kitchen and slammed one pot against another one. "You just see what she wants."

"And did you..." MayBelle leaned forward until she could feel her housecoat beginning to fall open at her throat. The old black woman's eyes cleared for an instant as if the milk had just reached a boil, then clouded again as she cut a look at the screen door to the kitchen, but not before MayBelle thought she could almost see into the center of them. There was a flash somewhere, a spark that flew up and burned out right before she could focus, like something she had remembered and not really seen at all.

Cora backed down to a lower step and stood stock-still, the

lard bucket held out in front of her. "I a Christian woman," she said, not moving. "I tell him to get on out from here. Get thee behind me, Satan."

The housecoat was hot, and as MayBelle pulled it closer around herself and looked off toward the ribbon of smoke hanging against the sky, she thought it was time to change to a dress in all this heat.

"I got some collards," Cora announced, shaking the lard bucket until it rustled. "I'm gone trade for some of Miss MayBelle's butter. That the sweetest there is."

"Cora, I told you lots of times before now I don't do nothing like that no more. I ain't had no cows in that pasture for years."

"Say you used to," Cora said, picking out a piece of trash from the collard greens and letting it drop beside the steps. It landed next to a doodle bug hole, and both women stood looking at it for a minute without saying anything.

"I can let you have a stick of oleo for them greens," MayBelle finally said and held out her hand.

"You got me a lard bucket?"

They made the trade, and MayBelle stood at the top of the steps watching the old woman pick her way back down the yard past the dog pen and up to the stile over the fence into the pasture. I believe that headrag is the map of Iowa or something, she told herself. Where would Cora get a thing like that?

"Can't you put these biscuits in the oven?" called Myrtle. "You know the doctor says I'm not supposed to make breakfast."

"Who all's going to the hospital, and who all's going to the drugstore?" asked Van Ray Cox, spinning around in the driver's seat of the Volkswagen van to peer into the back. "Hospital first. Y'all raise y'all's hands."

Van Ray had a full load this morning, five seniors and one retard, and all of them walkers. So there wouldn't be any need to break out the collapsible wheelchair he carried atop of the vehicle in a special rack his daddy had welded for him. It was a good job, solid quarter-inch pipe well-bonded and painted bright yellow and red to match the color of the van itself. Van Ray had made a special trip to Corrigan to get a sign man to paint the words on the side of the bus, and he felt like the extra trouble had been worth it. "Retired Seniors," it said in bright old English writing high up on both sides of the body. Below that was the word "Paraplegics" and under that were the large letters MR, which stood for "mentally retarded."

"But you don't want to actually come right out and say it just flat," he'd told the sign man. "It makes some folks nervous and might cost us some trade with people that ain't nuts."

But the lettering that Van Ray Cox and his partner Merle Lowe were proudest of was the slogan painted across the part of the van just over the big VW emblem. There the sign man had outdone himself, working with what he called a "distinguished Italian font." "We Serve the Unfortunate," stated the VW, coming at you, and on the back panel over the engine, going away from you.

"I don't like to brag," Van Ray said, to Merle on the day he brought the van back to Annette from the sign man, "but I do believe that there's the truth." He and Merle had to look off from each other at that moment because of the painful lumps rising up in their throats at the thought.

"It can't everybody be a preacher," Van Ray's daddy liked to say about his youngest son, "but of all my boys, Van Ray— he's the closest thing to it." And Van Ray didn't see any good reason to contradict the old man. Especially at night just before he dropped off to sleep when he liked to think over the good he had done during the day, picking up seniors and MR's, the odd old colored gentleman now and then, even sometimes driving all the way out to the Alabama-Coushatta Reservation to pick up a sick Indian or two to bring into town. It ain't only just the government allotments, he liked to tell himself, nor the extra little favors that matter.

So on the first Monday in August, after checking off the three seniors who had indicated they wanted to go to the hospital for examination, one of them having a good deal of trouble getting a hand up above shoulder level to signal that fact, Van Ray felt extra good as he dropped the VW into low gear and began working his way toward the middle of town. "Merle," he said into the CB microphone in his left hand, "this here's Vantastic. I'm carrying three seniors to Coushatta County Memorial and two seniors and a MR to Annette Drug. Ten-four."

Sitting between the retarded Ferguson girl and old Mrs. Gish, MayBelle slipped a hand down into her purse and felt for the prescription bottle and the five-dollar bill she had saved back from her check. Both were safe to hand, and she tried to lean back in the seat to catch some of the air coming through the side vent of the yellow and red van. One or the other of her seat companions made a contented gurgling sound, which one MayBelle couldn't tell, and both of them leaned in the same direction she was trying for. Worse than riding in Papa's old two-seated buggy, she thought, remembering how she had had to fight for room with Myrtle and Clytie on the way home from church on Sundays. It had generally ended up with her running along behind the buggy hanging on to the tailgate with one hand while she rubbed her eyes with the other one. At least until Myrtle started riding home with the Murphy boys and the Shugs and then all the other ones.

The VW was coming into downtown Annette now, and Van Ray Cox was saying something else on his radio. Red dust from the two-month-long drought lay over the parked cars and the store fronts and coated the signs at each corner. The flashing sign on top of the bank said it was 10:02 and 92 degrees, thanks for your patronage, but it had said that for the last two months and nobody believed it anymore. Up ahead a pulpwood truck had broken down, and two men were out looking under the hood, one of them poking at something underneath with a long screwdriver. As Van Ray crept by with less than a foot clearance, the other man, some kind of a Mexican, turned to look in the side window at the Ferguson girl who had pressed her face up against it to see out. He took one long look and then stuck his head back under the hood with the other man who was still poking away.

"It ain't no relief forecast," Van Ray Cox called over his shoulder to his load of passengers and craned his neck to look in the rearview mirror. "My radio says it ain't no sign of rain for the county, but they do expect some in Hardin and Tyler. Don't y'all wish you lived in one of them places?"

The ones of the seniors who could hear him allowed as how they did, and the rest asked MayBelle what the man had said. By the time the VW pulled into the circular drive at the rear of the Coushatta County Memorial Hospital she had managed to get the other two informed, but by then they didn't remember what they had asked her in the first place, and besides they were getting off here anyway.

Van Ray got the three hospital seniors unloaded and through the double doors, hustled his way back into the VW and pulled away for the Annette Pharmacy. Old man Ellis had left his Stetson in the back seat, Van Ray noticed, and would be asking every nurse, technician and doctor he saw where it was, but there wasn't time to take it in to him and still keep the schedule. Van Ray liked to pull up to the drugstore somewhere between seven and eight minutes after he had unloaded at the hospital, so he had to be moving right along.

He looked up into his rear view mirror to check the two remaining seniors and the MR and saw that MayBelle Holt was trying to catch his eye. He tipped her a big wink, and she leaned back in her seat satisfied and began looking out the side window again over the head of the MR beside her. Generally she waited until later in the week, but this was the Monday before the Big Caney graveyard working, and she likely had some fortifying to do. Like all seniors she had her special needs.

When he pulled up into the alley behind the Annette Pharmacy, Van Ray waited until the other senior and the MR had crawled out of the side door of the vehicle and walked into the store before he turned to MayBelle. She stood with one hand deep in her purse while she looked up and down the alley, but she shouldn't have been worried. Besides them, there was nobody behind the row of back doors except for a drunk Indian sitting on a pile of truck tires, and he was too far into a pint of vanilla extract to notice anything but the label on the bottle.

"Yes, ma'am," said Van Ray, beaming at the old lady in front of him. "The same as always?"

"Well," began MayBelle, "you're Ira's boy, aren't you?" She paused, looked at the drunk Indian, and went on in a faster voice. "I got five dollars this time, and I want to get the most I can for it. I don't mean bulk now. I mean strength." She looked at Van Ray over the tops of her glasses.

"Yessum, I got you," said Van Ray and held out his hand. "Just have it right there in the same place?"

MayBelle nodded, handed him the rolled-up bill and hurried on toward the door of the drugstore. "Keep some out for yourself," she said as she pulled at the metal door-handle.

"No problem, Miss Holt," Van Ray said and crawled up into the driver's seat to talk on his CB while the seniors and the retard filled their prescriptions.

Inside, the air was cool and smelled like chemicals, so MayBelle didn't mind waiting in line to hand her pill bottle to the Davis girl behind the counter. As she stood behind the retarded Ferguson girl, who was mumbling happily and stepping back and forth from one tile in the floor to the other, MayBelle looked around the shelves next to her. I flash. Do you? said words above the head of a half-naked girl on a cardboard sign right next to a shelf full of ointments and salves. The girl in the picture was wearing a bathing suit and a brown raincoat which she was holding open so a bunch of boys in bathing suits could see how tanned her skin was. MayBelle stood looking at the scene, carefully studying the face of each boy smiling at the girl's body, especially one whose mouth and nose reminded her of the way Jim Tolar used to look at the all-night fiddle dances back in Holly Springs. He had the same kind of grin back then, she thought, all them white teeth and no gums showing at all.

When was the last time I saw Jim, she wondered. Four or five graveyard workings ago with Betty and his four girls and grandkids at Big Caney. He smiles now, he shows plenty of gum, I reckon. She took a deep breath of the cool bitter-smelling air and tried to remember if they had spoken then, but couldn't, and then was comforted by the thought that Jim Tolar never had had much reason to smile at Betty any time in all the years he'd spent with her. "You want to buy you some of that Tanya Sunbutter, Miss MayBelle?"

The Davis girl was leaning across the counter, grinning and chewing Juicy Fruit gum, as she held out her hand for MayBelle's prescription bottle.

"I swear," said MayBelle, "that's a funny combination of clothes. A little old swimming suit and a raincoat." She turned to the counter and set the bottle in the Davis girl's hand.

"Is that what she's advertising? Sun tan salve? I couldn't tell for looking. No, I sure don't need me some of that stuff. I try to stay out of the sun, not get in it."

The woman took the bottle, walked back in between two long shelves of jars and tubes, and gave it to the druggist through a small window out into the back wall.

"How's Miss Myrtle?" she asked in a bright voice, her high heels clicking on the tile floor as she came back to face MayBelle across the counter.

"Fair to middling," said MayBelle. "Fair to middling. She don't get around much and she complains of hurting in her legs and back. She's getting a little old now, you know." She leaned across the sheet of glass in front of her and spoke in a lower voice for the Davis girl. "She's forgetful. Awful forgetful."

The Davis girl popped her gum, smiled and leaned back so that her chest lifted. "They get like that," she said. "Is her boy back in yet?"

"B.J's coming in today. Gonna be here all week for Big Caney."

"Uh huh," said the Davis girl. "Hi, Martha Sue." She waved a hand over MayBelle's head and opened her mouth so wide to grin that her gum came into view. "Lunch? Right. See you at Woolworth's at twelve."

She noticed MayBelle again and went back to the little window to pick up the prescription medicine, her skirt swishing as she walked and her hair bouncing with every step she took.

Outside, the dry heat hit her across the forehead like a hardwood club, and MayBelle raised both hands to her eyes to shade them, standing by the open door of the bus as Van Ray wrestled the senior and the MR back aboard. The Ferguson girl had not wanted to leave the cool store with its fascinating pattern of black and white floor tiles so she was whimpering as Van Ray tried to gentle her into the back seat. The senior already aboard reached out a shaking white hand and tried to pull at the girl's fingers, but she wasn't having any of it. She drew both hands back, crossed them over her chest and let her head sag so that she seemed to be trying to understand something interesting about the gravel of the alleyway.

"She's balked," said Van Ray, turning loose his hold and stepping away from the heavy girl. "Yep, she has sure to God balked on us."

MayBelle thought about trying to help and then decided against it. She looked down the alley at the Indian sitting on the truck tires. Since the occupants of the van had gone into the drugstore, the vanilla extract had taken a firmer purchase on the Indian's nervous system, and he had slumped back over the edge of the top tire and slipped partway into the hole in the middle. He rested now with fully two-thirds of his body folded up and slid down into the opening of the tire, his elbows crooked at each side to keep himself from falling any further in, and the soles of his shoes pointing up as though for inspection. They had a tread pattern on them, MayBelle noticed, and as she watched, she could see the left elbow slide off and the entire Indian take a slow tilt to that side. He held the extract bottle still in his right hand with a grip that seemed to be using up all the man had left of concentration. He lifted his arm to take the last swig left in the bottom of the bottle, and as he did, his tilt corrected itself and he slid the rest of the way on down into the tire.

"It's a lesson in that," said Van Ray Cox and turned back to grab hold of the MR again, but she had already crawled aboard the bus during the descent of the Indian and was bouncing up and down in the seat crooning to herself.

"Things take care of themselves sometimes," said MayBelle and got in the bus for the hot ride back home.

The Reverend B.J. Shackleford took the Oldsmobile into the last curve of Texas Highway 190 about a mile out of Annette at just under seventy miles per hour. When he came out into the last straightaway before the city limits the speedometer stood at a hair under eighty-two, and he immediately let off the accelerator and allowed the machine to slow of its own accord until he had dropped to fifty just as he crossed the line. It had been a good trip up from Corpus Christi. He had averaged sixty-seven miles per on the nose, the engine had not over-heated even though he had kept the air-conditioner on maximum all the way, and he had worked up the outline of a new sermon during the three hours coming in.

The text for the sermon had come to him as he waited for a redlight to change in Port Lavaca. The street was four lanes wide, and as he waited in the rightmost one, an orange convertible carrying two young women in shorts and halter tops had pulled up beside him and stopped, its motor revving and the muffler growling like a tomcat. B.J. looked over, caught the eye of the girl in the passenger seat, a brunette with a cigarette hanging between her lips, and gave her a big smile and a friendly howdy with lots of warmth in it. She leaned toward the girl at the wheel and said something, laughing, and then turned toward B.J. and stuck the middle finger of her right hand up at him, looking him straight in the eye during the whole operation.

The biblical reference came to B.J. just as the driver of the convertible popped the clutch and screeched off up the street, the backend of the car fishtailing for fully half a block as the oversized tires squealed. "The light of the body is the eye," ran the words in B.J.'s mind, and he repeated them as they passed through it. "If therefore thine eye be single, thy whole body shall be full of light."

Up ahead, the hair of the two harlots rippled and flashed in the wind as the orange convertible sped off, and B.J. sat still in his Oldsmobile feeling the power of the Word until a GMC pickup behind him honked because the light was green.

He didn't get the Olds above twenty for the next seven or eight miles he was so occupied in sorting out the main topics of the sermon he would build from this chance meeting with the little whores of Lavaca. It would go over like gangbusters, as his old Baptist Seminary teacher used to say, when he got a chance to use it. Maybe he could fit it in at the graveyard working at Big Caney, he had thought, and let the Olds unwind several notches.

Now as B.J. eased on through Annette toward Mama's house, he looked from one side of the familiar street to the other one: past the junior high school, the big brick church of the First Methodists, the smaller frame structure of the Cathedral of the Unentombed Christ, the trailer homes scattered here and there between the duplexes and the three-room shotgun houses. Everywhere he looked the red dust lay thick and unmoving in the noon fire of the sun, and all the trees drooped, even the needles of the loblolly and long-leaf pines. Everything looked blistered. Oh, it was going to be a hot dry week in Coushatta County for him, he said to himself, leaning forward to scan the dials, needles, and air-conditioning vents ranged along the sweep of the Oldsmobile dashboard.

It was a pure hardship to have to leave the lush wet coast of Corpus Christi and its freon-cooled houses and sanctuaries and come all the way up here to the two-month-long drought which had settled into East Texas, but he had to do it every two weeks for the guard dogs and this time for the graveyard working at Big Caney too. He hoped Mama would at least have some electric fans going, and he took comfort from the thought that the dogs anyway would be mean and edgy from all this sun and dust.

No cars were parked in the driveway running beside the house, so B.J. was able to pull the Olds almost all the way into the backyard before he had to stop. He cut the engine and sat there for a minute in the cool, looking over at the dog pen before he cracked the door, picked up the Bible that always rode shotgun beside him in the passenger seat, and stepped out into the Coushatta County summer heat.

The backdoor to Mama's house opened and B.J. waved the Bible in that direction without looking and walked over to the hogwire enclosure. The five German shepherds lying in the shade of the mimosa by the fence turned their heads to watch him, but not a one of them raised a hackle or made a sound. The three Dobermans were over in the far corner, setting on their haunches in a circle facing in, but none of them made a sign that they had even seen him.

"Mama," B.J. said to the shuffling sound coming up behind him, "Mama, I wish you'd look at these guard dogs."

"Son," said Myrtle, "them's nice seersucker pants. Where'd you get them? At Sears or Penney's down yonder in Corpus?" She came up and touched him on the seat pocket, and B.J. moved away a step.

"I don't want to talk about these pants that Peachie bought for me," he said in a strangled voice. "I want to know why these guard dogs ain't meaner. They wouldn't bite a biscuit if you put gravy on it." He gestured toward the circle of Dobermans, and at the movement one of the shepherds made a comfortable groaning sound deep in its throat.

"I mean just look at them. Don't they even fight each other no more? I don't see sign one of a mark on any of them."

"You say Peachie bought them for you? She always can pick out the best looking clothes for you and the children." Myrtle stopped talking and reached out for the pocket again. "But this pair is a little tight across the hips, ain't they?"

B.J. kicked the hogwire with his left foot and shifted his Bible to the other hand. "Mama, I already been through this before with you and Aunt MayBelle. If I'm going to be able to branch out some from preaching and get into the physical protection business, I'm going to have to be able to show some vicious mean-tempered dogs to people to break into the market. Why, do you know what a Mexican or a hippie crazy on dope would do to one of them, them..." He stopped to think of the right term for the passive animals, couldn't find it and jerked the Bible into the air over his head with a disgusted look on his face.

"I know, honey, I know," said Myrtle. "I try to get MayBelle to work on them, but she won't hardly do nothing I tell her anymore anyhow."

B.J. had brought the eight dogs in front of them up to Annette about six months ago, after he had decided the trouble they were causing him in Corpus Christi was too intense. The whole enterprise had seemed a wonderful idea when he first thought of it, and he still believed in its fundamental wisdom. Crime is getting worse and worse every day, he had told Alton Mosser, the head deacon of the Second Baptist Church which B.J. pastored in Corpus, and it seems like the head of a family can't go to sleep at night with any assurance that he won't wake up the next morning and find his wife and babies slaughtered in their beds by some doped-up hippie or wetback and all his valuables gone to buy more pot and pills.

B.J. had conceived the idea one night after watching the Big Ten Roundup of News on Channel 10, Corpus. Hugh Bill, the newscaster, had told of a Marine sergeant somewhere in Florida whose house had been invaded by a gang of hippies who had chopped the mother of the family to death with a machete and drowned the children and the cat in the downstairs bathroom.

B.J. had immediately set down the rootbeer float he was drinking and offered up a prayer for the poor Marine, a man just back from Vietnam where he had seen such atrocities as to cause him to be granted extended medical leave with his family. "Lord," he had prayed, kneeling there by the recliner rocker with Peachie at his side, "what can we do to keep Satan from working this kind of evil in Corpus Christi?" And it was at that moment, there between the Barcalounger and the TV set, that B.J. was granted the answer.

Help for God's people, warnings for them when evil is nigh, something to protect them from the foe that comes creeping and silent in the night.

"Christian Guard Dogs," B.J. said out loud. "German shepherds and Dobermans trained and sold to Christians by a preacher of the gospel." He had turned to Peachie, hugged her and given her a full kiss of love. "Honey," he said, "I found it. We're going to make some real money out of this."

He began by investing one thousand dollars of his own money and two thousand of Deacon Moss's in a couple of hundred feet of heavy-duty chain, a dozen tempered steel stakes, and eight German shepherd and five Doberman puppies. A member of his congregation who raised Santa Gertrudis cattle on a little ranch south of Palacios gave B.J. an electric cattle prod, and at that point the pastor of the Corpus Christi Second Baptist Church considered Christian Guard Dogs, Incorporated to be in business.

But raising and training the killer dogs in the backyard of the parsonage immediately began presenting problems, some minor and several major. First off, during the first night after B.J. and his oldest boy had hammered the tempered steel stakes into the half-acre of yard just the other side of Peachie's rose bushes and fastened each dog to its own chain, one of the Dobermans slipped his collar and killed three of the German shepherd puppies, pausing to eat only part of one of them before leaving for unknown regions. B.J. discovered his first losses the next morning when, dressed in the heavy quilted suit, he went out with the cattle prod to begin training the puppies to grow up and protect Christians. And by the time he buried the shepherds and finished the first session with the cattle prod, one of the Dobermans had got too excited and passed away from a heart attack or a stroke or some kind of a fit.

B.J. had been allowing the little black square-headed animal to grab ahold of his padded left arm, and then he had stuck the cattle prod to the underside of its throat while the animal groaned and foamed at his arm. After one particularly fierce charge at the padded quilting, the Doberman had got a good solid purchase and was shaking its head back and forth in a frenzy as it worried what it had in its jaws. B.J. jammed the business end of the cattle prod into the fur at the point of the dog's left jaw and really let him have a jolt, but the animal refused to let go and after a minute or so of electric shock keeled over shaking, jerking and finally dying in a heap.

"Well, Peachie," B.J. said to the mother of his children, "the little fellow was game. He had the courage of David but he just couldn't take it long enough." He looked sadly down at the dead Doberman and poked it with his foot. "Better to discover it now, I guess, rather than have it fail some Christian in his moment of physical need."

But the event that finally made it necessary for B.J. to send Christian Guard Dogs, Inc. to East Texas for the toughening-up period had to do not with unexpected losses of personnel, but with a nosy neighbor up the street, who was either a lapsed Presbyterian or an atheist. His name was Coleman Beasley. He drove a dirty-colored Volkswagen bug, and he never trimmed the weeds along the fence line separating his property from the people next door.

One Sunday afternoon between dinner and the time B.J. had to go into his study to pray for guidance before preaching the evening sermon, he had looked up from working one of the shepherds and seen Coleman Beasley watching him from his back fence two yards down. B.J. had lifted the cattle prod at him in greeting and gone back to his business and thought no more about it. He remembered the way Beasley didn't wave back, though, the next day when he got the telephone call at the church office from the Society for the Prevention of Cruelty to Animals.

The woman on the other end had threatened him with a visit from the sheriff's office, an injunction and a story in the *Corpus Christi Coast News*. She had refused to listen to his explanation of the aims of Christian Guard Dogs, Inc. and his description of training methods used by teachers of protective dogs. "It's all just part of a system of agitation," he had been explaining into the telephone when she had hung up on him. So the next weekend in a dark mood of sorrow at the unwillingness of people to listen to Christian reason, B.J. had loaded the eight remaining dogs into a U-Haul trailer and pulled them behind the Oldsmobile, growling and snapping at each other, to Annette to carry on with the project.

"Well, Mama," he said, looking at the trunk of the Olds and then back toward the dogs panting behind the hogwire, "I see I've got my work cut out for me this week."

"I know you do, honey," said Myrtle, shading her eyes as she looked deep into the pen. "Just don't let none of them mean things bite you."

"I hope they *are* mean by the time the graveyard working gets here," B.J. said. "I brought some fresh batteries for the cattle prod with me. I bet the ones in it have corroded and turned green."

"I can't depend on MayBelle for a thing," said his mother, shuffling over to the Olds in a series of small steps and peering through the tinted glass into the backseat. "She won't even cook a mess of peas anymore, much less work with your Christian guard dogs." She stopped and leaned closer to the side window. "What's that big thing in the floorboard? Is it some new curtains Peachie sent to me?"

"A tent, Mama," said B.J. "It's a mountaineer's tent. I figured me and Barney Lee might camp out a couple of nights in it while I'm up here. You still got my Coleman lantern?"

"It's around here somewhere, I reckon," Myrtle said and turned back to face the house. The German shepherd nearest

23

the fence got up from the red dust of the pen, sniffed at a dry water bowl and lifted its leg against one of the posts. A couple of drops hung on the fence wire and glistened in the sun.

"You're not gonna go way off in the woods to camp, are you, son?"

"No," said B.J. and watched the sprinkling of shepherd piss dwindle and disappear. "You know I've got to be convenient to a bathroom. We'll just pitch the tent close to the old treehouse." He looked into the backyard at a loblolly pine next to a chinaberry tree. The needles on the top limbs had turned brown and brittle from the drought and all but two of the plank supports of the treehouse had rotted away from the nails holding them.

"If Barney Lee's in Annette," B.J. said to the two by fours of the treehouse.

"He's here, all right, honey," said Myrtle. "He's got so fat with that bad back that he can't stand to drive anywhere. He don't even try to preach anymore."

"What's he doing then, Mama?"

"All he *can* do is watch television and eat. He does pray a lot, his mama tells me. Sometime he'll go on half the night talking out loud with the Lord." Myrtle shook her head sadly. "He's just fat, fat," she said.

B.J. and Barney Lee had grown up together in Annette, gone to school in the same grade, and been saved the same night. Old Brother Searce Percy, the preacher that night at the Annette First Baptist, liked to tell about it later: "It looked to me up there behind the pulpit like B.J. and Barney Lee were in a race up that aisle to profess their faith in the saving power of Jesus's blood. Oh, it was an amusing, but an inspiring sight to see those young comrades, later to be preachers themselves, come almost running up that aisle of salvation."

Barney Lee Richards had always tried to do everything B.J. did, and the dedication to Christian service was no different.

They had even gone off to college together, up there to Marshall to East Texas Bible Institute, but somewhere along the way Barney Lee had faltered in the tough world of academic study and fallen by the wayside. Unlike B.J., who finished at Eastex Bible and went on to the Baptist Seminary, Barney had dropped out the second year and answered the call to preach at a little country church in Colmesneil. He never had been able to keep up, but B.J. was glad to overlook his weaknesses and loved to see Barney Lee whenever he could. He was looking forward to the night or two he might be able to spend with his old friend, there in the backyard in the mountaineer's tent, praying and reminiscing together under the old treehouse they had built together many years before. B.J. hoped Barney Lee hadn't gotten so fat he couldn't fit into a close place like a canvas tent with drawstring doors.

"Mama," said B.J., "I think I'll go get cleaned up, maybe eat a little something, and then come out and agitate these dogs."

Behind the hogwire fence the Dobermans still sat in the same inward-looking circle, but another of the German shepherds had risen from the dust to check out one of the posts. By the time B.J. and Myrtle reached the front door to the house the other three shepherds had joined the two already up rummaging in the feed and water bowls. One of them growled at another one that had gotten in its way, but not loud enough to get snapped at.

From where she stood at the sink in the kitchen MayBelle could hear Myrtle and B.J. coming into the house, Myrtle speaking in a low voice so MayBelle couldn't hear and B.J. answering her in one- and two-word sentences. MayBelle finished the plate she was washing, rinsed it under the faucet and stacked it in the drain-rack. It was a blue pattern with red flowers that had faded to a whitish pink, and looking at it there, wet beside the dish rack, MayBelle decided to pick it up and let it slip through her fingers to break on the floor. She did that, picked up the three parts into which it had cracked and threw them into a brown paper sack under the sink.

"Is that B.J. I hear a talking?" she called out loud and wiped her hands on her apron. She met him in the dining room and hugged him close enough to smell his hair oil and then backed off to look up at him. "You're just as tall as your daddy was," she told B.J.

"That's what you always say, Aunt MayBelle," he said, "and it's still not right." He was looking off to one side, not meeting her eyes, and he was fanning his face with his Bible.

"You know how long it's been now, B.J?" asked Myrtle from the living room where she had sat down in one of the rockers.

"How long, Mama?" said B.J. "Where's that electric fan we gave you and Aunt MayBelle for Christmas?" He looked around the room and craned to see through the door into the kitchen. "It was here two weekends ago."

"It's been twelve years this week. It was the very day before Big Caney twelve years ago." Myrtle let her voice fade out into a kind of choke on the last syllable and pointed with her right hand toward the green overstuffed sofa along one wall of the living room beneath the picture of the field of bluebonnets.

"I'd give anything to see Burton Shackleford lying there right now looking at that television," said Myrtle and rocked back in the chair until both of her feet lifted off the floor and then came back down with a slap.

For the last eight years of his life, Burton had spent about two-thirds of his waking hours resting on the green sofa, the big Dumont console TV tuned to one of the Houston channels, watching whatever the program managers saw fit to send out over the airwaves. He was Myrtle's second husband, the father of her children, and he figured at age sixty-five he had fought the good fight, he had finished the course, he had kept the faith. The first husband had walked out on Myrtle one day about a year after the wedding, wearing a brand-new Panama straw hat and leaving her pregnant with a baby she was lucky enough to miscarry two days later. Myrtle had married Burton in 1931 after a chance meeting in the Courthouse Cafe in Leggett and a whirlwind courtship driving down Highway 59 toward Annette.

So after spending half his working years raising three children and putting up with his wife's sister right there the whole time in the house, Burton Shackleford had retired to the green sofa and the Dumont. It had been a varied career for him: short order cook in his nephew's restaurant in Dry Creek, night watchman for the T.&N.O. Railroad, and manager for the Billups station out on the Woodville Highway until the Negro gunmen had run him out. "They got to where they wouldn't take no for an answer," Burton liked to say, "and when that big fat black woman came in with a Stevens Four-Ten shotgun on my sixty-fifth birthday I was glad to give it up to the next fellow."

He had earned the years on the green sofa, he figured, and he had lain there smoking Lucky Strikes, now and then changing the dial, listening to the cars pass on the road and the pinecones fall on the roof in a state of perfect satisfaction right up until that last Saturday evening. Curly Fox and Texas Ruby had just finished singing a duet number, *May the Circle be Unbroken*, and a commercial was coming on when Burton took a big drag off his cigarette, coughed deep in his throat and fell back dead. Myrtle knew in her bones he was gone when she didn't hear the channel selector click over to six after Curly and Texas Ruby sang the theme song ending their show.

Burton's last cigarette burned a little hole in the back of the sofa where he had let his arm fall, and it was mainly to hide the spot that Myrtle now kept a light-blue cover spread over the piece of furniture. From where she habitually set in the oak rocker she could still see the shiny marks on the wooden arm of the sofa where Burton's shoes had worn away the varnish during his eight years there, and she liked being able to glance over at the marks whenever she felt like it. For a few years after Burton had slipped back for good into a reclining position, she would tell herself that he was just gone to the bathroom or to get a drink of water or a new pack of Luckies from the carton he kept by the bed, but she had stopped doing that on a regular basis after a while. And now it was only very occasionally she needed to tell herself anything like that at all.

"Let's look in the back rooms," MayBelle said to B.J. "It's probably been drug off in there by somebody."

"Son," Myrtle called from the rocker, "you going to pray with me in here now, won't you?"

"Not now, Mama. After a while I will," B.J. answered, following MayBelle through the doorway into the hall and past the bathroom.

"I meant after you find the fan," said Myrtle in a louder voice.

"She's hard of hearing and getting worse," MayBelle said and pointed to the electric fan in the back bedroom. "Yonder it is where Sis left it."

B.J. nodded and laid his Bible on the dresser beside the fan. "Anything to eat, Aunt MayBelle?" he asked, heading back toward the kitchen. He just put his hand right on the mark on the door facing and doesn't even know anything about it, MayBelle thought to herself and followed her nephew into the next room. It's just part of an old door facing to him, nothing more than that.

"It's some banana pudding," she said.

When MayBelle came out the back door and walked across the yard toward the road, Bubba Shackleford was standing by his pickup with one foot up on the running board, watching his big brother beginning to work the Christian guard dogs. Bubba had sweated through his shirtback driving his pickup in the heat of the day, and he had a worried look on his face.

"Hidy, Aunt MayBelle," he said. "Hot enough for you?" He wiped his shirtsleeve across his face and hitched his khaki pants up over his belly, but they wouldn't stay put again. The red dust had streaked the door of his pickup so thickly that it was hard to read the sign on the side, and Bubba was standing so that the width of his body blocked most of it. MayBelle knew what it read, though: Shackleford's Septic Tank Service and a telephone number she never could remember.

"I reckon it is," she said. "It's still this hot this late in the day." She put up her parasol and, not looking toward the dog pen, walked out to the road and turned to the right. Behind her she heard a dog yip, and she picked up her step a little, looking straight in front toward where the Sunflower Road bent a quarter of a mile away beyond a stand of sweet-gum trees. Up ahead, the asphalt of the roadbed shimmered in the heat, and the sun cast a long shadow of her and the parasol off to the side among the parched weeds in the ditch.

MayBelle gave herself over to walking and tried to hum a tune in her head to keep her mind occupied until she reached the turn in the road. Two cars and a gasoline truck had passed by the time she got close, sending waves of hot air and dust washing over her and causing her parasol to list way to the side. The asphalt was tacky in the heat, and she stepped carefully in the gravel of the road shoulder to avoid getting any of the melted tar on her shoes. Next time I look up, she thought, I'll be there. And when she lifted her eyes she saw the grove of sweet gum not over fifty feet away, a brown rabbit sitting in the shadow at the edge of the line of trees, its sides rapidly moving in and out as it rested in the dry air. It hopped off slowly into the woods, after she'd taken three or four more steps, leaving a little cloud of dust hanging in the air behind it.

"Too hot and dry even for the varmints," MayBelle said aloud and, not breaking her stride, lowered the parasol and made a little jump down into the dusty bar ditch beside Sunflower Road. She walked another twenty feet and then bent over to look into the mouth of the culvert opening off the side of the ditch. The road crew had buried a thirty-six inch corrugated pipe beneath the road years ago, and it was beginning to corrode and rust out where the water took its usual path through it. It was dry as a bone now, though, and it looked cool and dark up inside the pipe. MayBelle picked up a couple of small rocks and gingerly tossed them into the opening, and then she leaned over, her shoes slipping a little in the gravel ditchbed, and thrust her parasol inside to rattle around a little. She stopped to listen, breath held and eyes fixed on the culvert, but could hear no sound. There seemed to be nothing inside to bite her, so she lowered herself to her knees and reached as far as she could into the culvert, feeling along the right side of the rusting pipe for the hole that had been eaten away by the elements. What she was looking for was there, and she drew it out into the light.

Van Ray Cox had gotten her the white-colored this time, and MayBelle reached into her purse for her glasses to read the label. Depending on the price of things at Arden Hooks' place just across the Trinity River, Van Ray was liable to bring back about anything from the little buying trips he made for various people in and around Annette. Most of them weren't particular, as long as it was cheap enough and strong enough to get the job done, so Van Ray purchased whatever was most economical. Once he had brought MayBelle back a fifth of heavy yellow liquid that poured almost like honey and that she had had to cut with Pepsi Cola about half and half before she could get it down. And it had gagged her so that she could barely force herself to drink enough of it at one time to get the full benefit. Another trip had resulted in a bottle of what was called Southern Comfort, a sweet sticky clear stuff, that went down almost like Kool Aid, but that had a two-day stun packed away somewhere in it. Mainly, though, what Van Ray found on sale were pints of various fruit brandies, the odd bottle of tequila with the label all in Mexican, various bourbons and bourbon imitations, a bottle or two of creme de menthe, and other cut-rate leavings of consignments first delivered to the big Houston outlets which had eventually worked their way down to Arden Hooks' Fish Camp and Package Store just across the line in Angelina County.

This time what MayBelle was holding up to the last rays of the sun was a bottle of clear liquid with a label in some kind of a foreign language. Puzzled, she turned the quart bottle from side to side to try to see something familiar but was able to pick out only one word that looked like anything she had seen or heard of before. *Wodka*, the label said under the picture of a large bear with a doglike head which bore a kind of a crown. It's Russian liquor, MayBelle told herself, looking hard at the Bear-King fitted with a muzzle like a bluetick hound. It's some kind of a communist whiskey. She stuffed the bottle down into her black plastic purse and started to stand up in the bar ditch but had to wait until a car passed, blowing clouds of red clay dust out both sides. "I bet this booster's mighty strong," she said to the darkness in the culvert's mouth and climbed up out of the ditch, her purse tight under her left arm and its strap firm across her shoulder.

"Yonder comes Aunt MayBelle back," said Bubba Shackleford to B.J. "Wonder where she's been?"

B.J. didn't answer. He had donned the thick padded suit and a baseball catcher's mask, and he was now leaning over the

31

hogwire fence with a long pole with a wire noose attached to one end poking at the biggest one of the Dobermans. He was having a hard time getting the dog to lift its head so the noose could slip over, sweat was pouring from underneath the quilted suit like ice water off a glass, and the elastic straps of the Johnny Bench catcher's mask felt like they were cutting off circulation to the top of his head.

B.J. stepped back and caught a big breath of dead air. He pulled the mask off his head, leaned the catch pole against his brother's pickup bed and looked over at the Doberman. It was sitting up now with its head in a perfect capture position, studying the two men on the other side of the hogwire, its eyes yellow and unblinking.

"He's sure a pretty thing, ain't he?" said Bubba, prodding at the dogpen and looking worried.

"Yeah, Bubba," B.J. said, "but is he ever going to be mean enough? Is this thing going to pay off for me?"

"I's you, I wouldn't worry about it," Bubba answered, shifting his feet and picking with his teeth at a thumbnail. "Things always work out for you all right. Me, I have my troubles."

"What's wrong, little brother? Business again?" B.J. tried to speak in the tone he would use with one of his congregation back in Corpus Christi, but it didn't sound exactly right. He tried it again. "Is it problems of this world?"

"I tell you, B.J.," said Bubba, "this day and age the onliest problem a man in the septic tank service has is of this world. This un here's the only world they is for a septic tank man." Bubba looked pensive and spit out some thumbnail pieces.

"Thing is, see, the city is spreading them sewer lines everywhere, and they got a law that everybody's got to hook up with them. That don't leave me much show."

"You don't get to put in many new septic tanks then?" B.J. asked and reached down for the Johnny Bench mask.

"Not a one in town anywhere. The only ones'll buy septic tanks these days is a dirt farmer now and then." Bubba stopped for a minute and looked off at the red ball of fire sinking in the west. "And most of them'd still just as soon make big potty in the woods."

"Uh huh," said B.J., beginning to adjust his straps and buttons.

"Waste handling is important," Bubba announced in a firm voice and held out his right arm as though he were addressing a convention of septic tank servicers. "And the septic tank is nature's most efficient way of handling waste." He turned toward his big brother, now almost fully ready for battle with the Christian guard dogs again, and seized his arm.

"Do you know, B.J.," he said, "them microbes has they best chance to work when the number one and number two is setting still in one place, not sloshing up and down some plastic pipes under the street." He looked B.J. full in the Johnny Bench mask and asked in a slow earnest tone, "How can human waste rot and disintegrate when it's moving? I ask you, you're a preacher been to college. You talk to people everyday that know all kind of stuff. Have you ever had anybody argue with you in your whole ministry that human waste will rot better a moving? Now just tell me if you did."

B.J. patted his brother on the shoulder with a thick glove and allowed as how he never did.

"Because one thing I know, "said Bubba, "and I never went to college, is human waste products. It's different kinds, B.J., and it all decays at its own rate."

B.J. had picked up the catch pole and was moving toward the fence, catcher's mask in place, and noose loosened for action. Bubba came away from the pickup to intercept him, talking as he trotted after his bother. "Do you know, B.J.," he was saying, "that the poop of a white man, a Mexican and a nigger has all got different rates of decay? Yeah. And it depends on the age and the sex too. And what they been eating."

About then B.J. managed to slip the wire noose over the head of the Doberman on his first try, and he was so surprised and happy that he leaned back on the pole hard enough he almost lifted the dog off the ground.

"Open that gate, Bubba," he said. "I'm fixing to bring him out."

"She's open," said Bubba, lifting the gate hasp and stepping well back out of the way. The Doberman came reluctantly toward the gap in the fence, tongue out and eyes bulging, as B.J. hauled away with the catch pole. A couple of the other prospective guard dogs got up to see what was happening, but none of them showed any inclination to try to leave the pen. When it reached the gate itself the Doberman dug all four feet in and sat back on its haunches, but B.J. managed to get some leverage against a post and prized the dog on out into the open yard.

"The Lord be praised," he said, "it's outside. Close that gate and hand me that cattle prod lying there on the ground, Bubba."

"You got it, big brother," said Bubba, whipping the hasp closed and picking up the three-foot-long electric encourager. On the end of the device, raised letters painted over in red spelled out the company slogan: Get Along Little Dogie.

"This thing hot?" asked Bubba.

"It ought to be. I just put in brand new batteries."

The Reverend Shackleford took the end of the catch pole away from the dog while he got ready to work him.

"Our Loving Father," he said tilting the Johnny Bench mask toward the ground and touching the fingers of his heavy gloves together in front of his chest, "bless me in this agitation of Thy Doberman and lead this animal to save them and Thy children in their moment of physical need for protection. May Christian Guard Dogs, Incorporated prosper financially and protectively, if it be Thy will." He looked up through the slit in the catcher's mask toward the line of pines at the far horizon, fell silent for a couple of beats, and then intoned in a firm voice, "Amen."

"Bubba," he said, "you watch this," and then hit the Doberman just at the tip of the muzzle with a thirty-volt shot.

"Oh wee, look at him jump," said Bubba, the catch pole jerking up and down in his hands as the animal swerved, trembled and chewed at the air. "He's gonna be a good one, ain't he?"

"Well, I pray he will be," B.J. answered and moved around to get a better angle for his next application.

By the time he had finished with the three Dobermans and the first of the German shepherds, all eight dogs were snapping and growling at each other, at the hogwire fence, and at the cluster of neighborhood children from across the road who had congregated in the gathering darkness to see what was causing all the commotion. Bubba was dead-tired from hanging on to the end of the catch pole and was beginning to complain about shooting pains in his forearms and shoulders, and B.J. himself had sweated through the quilted attack suit and the leather of the Johnny Bench mask.

"Let me finish with this one," he said to Bubba, hitting the switch again on the cattle prod, "and we'll get the other three early in the morning."

It had been a good afternoon's work, and B.J. knew the three he hadn't been able to agitate today would be bothered enough during the night by the five he'd already treated to be almost as mean and snappish in the morning as the veterans were. Bubba had been a lot of help to him, and he promised himself to give his little brother the benefit of his attention in a good family conference as a payment later or sometime.

"The soul of a man comes first," he told Bubba as they put the shepherd back in the pen, "but you know exercise makes you realize the importance of the body. It's the temple of the spirit, the Book tells us."

"That's right," said Bubba, hitching his pants up and sticking his shirt down inside all around as he talked. "And you realize that the waste of the human body is a testimony too." He slammed one hand into the other one for emphasis. "It's *got* to have a chance to sit here and fester, like it can do in a septic tank." He went on, his eyes blazing as he looked up into his brother's face, "It just cannot decompose like it ought to, being washed on down a six-inch plastic pipe."

MayBelle flipped the blouse over, adjusted it on the board and started on one of the sleeves. The material was heavy and needed some more water so she picked up the Windex bottle she had converted into a sprayer and squirted a couple of pumps of mist into the cloth. The hot iron slid easily up and down the board, sending a light cloud of steam up from the cloth, and she leaned over it to sniff some of the warm air into her nose. It made her want to sneeze so she stopped for a minute, her mouth open and her eyes half-closed, to wait for it to come. She could hear the steady sound from the living room of Myrtle's rocker lightly surging back and forth on the hardwood floor as she sat in front of the Dumont, watching either the Newlywed Game or the Seven-Hundred Club. The voices of the announcers were no different, and the happy sounds of the two audiences were enough alike to make it hard to distinguish between the two shows at a distance. Somebody on the set let out a squeal, either of joy or conviction, and she still couldn't tell which show it was Myrtle was experiencing.

Myrtle had always been hell-bound to listen in to the airwaves, whatever was coming over them, either the television signals or, back before they came to East Texas, the radio shows that she picked up on her series of sets. She had begun when they were little girls living on Papa's place out at Holly Springs in the big double log house with the dog trot running down through the middle of it. One of the Stutts boys had given her a radio that ran on big red batteries, and as soon as Myrtle got that tuned in, she had not done much else but listen to it until she finally ran off with Whit Lollar to Houston for that eleven months.

When she came back without Whit, the main thing she was toting with her aside from a few clothes was a radio that plugged into a wall-socket and picked up music, funny shows and baseball games from all over. The radio's electrical requirement was the main reason she had moved into a garage apartment in Annette and not back to Holly Springs. She had got MayBelle to leave Papa's house and move in with her to help out while she worked in Creamer's Department Store downtown, and that had been it.

MayBelle Holt had started cooking for her sister, washing and ironing, cleaning house, answering the telephone, and churning butter, and she was still at it.

Her sneeze finally came, and a commercial started up in the television in the living room, a man talking about a new machine that would do any and every thing to a potato. Myrtle said something back to the man and stopped rocking for a minute.

After this next sleeve, MayBelle decided, sliding the iron around the button, I'm going to start in on that bottle of communist whiskey.

The mountaineer's tent was giving B.J. and Barney Lee Richards a hard time in the backyard. They were working to set the shelter up by the light coming from a single bulb on the porch, and that wasn't nearly enough to see the plastic tent pegs they were trying to drive into the hard baked clay with B.J.'s camping hatchet. Mama was right about Barney Lee. He had become fat enough not to want to bend over except in emergencies, and his added weight made him gasp for breath at the slightest exertion. He now sat with his legs spraddled in the dust of the backyard with the end of a tentrope in his hand, trying to keep things rigid while B.J. drew back to hit at an invisible peg which was supposed to glow in the dark, according to the manufacturer's claim.

"You know why we ain't being eaten up by mosquitoes?" he asked B.J. and shifted his hips to get off of a pinecone gouging him in the rump.

"Why's that?" said B.J. "Too hot for them?"

"That's right, Brother B," Barney said, trying to tighten his hand to keep the slick plastic from sliding between his fingers. "We going on the sixty-fourth day of this drought. All the water in the country is dried up. People have been seeing things come up out of the woods to look for water. They finding foxes and deer drinking right along with the livestock in the lot."

"Tighter on that rope some more. I'm about to get this one started."

"All right," Barney Lee said and put his other hand on the plastic. "It can't nothing much make it in this heat without water." B.J. got in a lick with the hatchet, and some of the rope tension eased in Barney Lee's hand. After another couple of blows on the tent pegs, he was able to let the rope go altogether and he began to rock from side to side so he could get turned over on his belly and be able to use both arms to get himself worked up to a standing position.

"That sun starts at six in the morning. It don't let up all day. And there ain't a cloud in the sky, and not hardly a puff of breeze all day neither." Barney Lee stopped talking to devote full attention to the last stages of getting to his feet and finally made it, swaying back and forth for balance with both arms held out to catch his breath. The dust raised by his efforts rose around him like a fogbank, swirling in the yellow porch light and giving Barney Lee the appearance of a blind bear caught in a sandstorm.

"Let's get on in the tent," B.J. said in a kind tone. "I'll get the lantern and your Bible for you."

Barney Lee dropped heavily to the ground again, landing on his knees and starting to crawl toward the tent opening, and by the time B.J. got back with the lantern, a thermos of coffee, a bag of Oreo cookies, and his and Barney's Bibles, he had crawled into the far end of the tent and flopped over to rest on his right side, the one farthest from his heart.

"Brother B," he said, "it's gonna be hot in here."

"Not once we get to praying and the Lord moves," said B.J. "God'll cool things down."

The two old comrades in Christ, as Dr. Percy had called them, lay in the tent quietly for a few minutes, the only sound a car or two passing by on Sunflower Road and from across the back pasture the cry of a hoot owl hunting field mice. Through the tent flap B.J. could see one dim light down in the quarter, and as he watched, it flickered and went out.

"Other than the graveyard working and the drought, what's the news around Coushatta County nowadays, Brother B. Lee?" he asked, looking in the dark tent toward the sound of Oreo's being eaten.

"Nothing much," said Barney Lee and paused for a long time, "except I think I'm losing my faith." He made a sobbing sound in his throat and crunched up another mouthful of cookies.

B.J. sat silent in the mountaineer's tent, astounded, a Bible in his hand and a sick feeling just below his chestbone. He didn't believe he had heard what he knew he had. A Baptist preacher, even one who had flunked out of Eastex Bible, didn't do such things as what Barney Lee had just given voice to. At worst he might start speaking in tongues and sink to being a preacher to some sort of pentecostal holy roller outfit, or in

more cases than that he might move up socially and become a
Methodist or once in a great while a Presbyterian. But a Baptist
who had had the call to go forth and preach the gospel just
didn't start believing he was losing faith itself.

"Is it a woman, Barney Lee?" he finally said in a careful
voice after a full two minutes of alternately tracing his finger-
tips over the pebbled leather covering his Bible and pulling at
a loose thread in a seam of the tent.

"Naw," said Barney Lee. "I wished it was something as easy
as that. And it ain't my overeating neither. I know lots of
overweight preachers, and they ain't bothered none." He took
a deep bubbly breath and let it out in a groan with a whistle in
it. "It's something in the air. I can smell it in the morning when
I wake up and at night when I'm going off to sleep. It's kinda
like the way milk is when it's going sour. I smell it even when
I'm dreaming. I smell it all the time. I can smell it right now in
this mountaineer's tent."

Barney Lee gave another groan and rolled over against the
cloth wall until the plastic ropes sung, and then he rolled back
to the other side of the shelter until the ropes there did the same
thing. He ended up with his face against the tent wall, breathing
what little air there was between him and the rubberized
groundcloth in great suffering gulps.

"Barney Lee," said B.J., looking down at his old friend and
speaking in a deep comforting voice, "you don't sound to me
like you've lost your faith. You act to me like a man who has
come under conviction."

"No, it ain't conviction. I done looked it up and read about
it over and over. It's what that World Book Encyclopedia calls
despair."

Barney Lee was now struggling to sit up in the tent, his arms
splayed out to each side as he heaved his upper body forward
into an upright position.

"You can look it up yourself, too, B.J.," he was saying. "It's in that F volume under faith. It says it's an old problem going all the way back to the beginning, despair is. And you know what else it says, B.J.?" Barney Lee stopped to wait for an answer, sitting up all the way by now and trying to get a good deep breath so he could open his throat up a little.

"What does the World Book say?" B.J. finally said, looking at the dark shape looming in the back of the tent.

"It says," said Barney Lee, quoting the heavy words as exactly as he could, "it says that some religious sources consider it to be the unpardonable sin." He said the last two words as carefully as a man sucking at a bad jaw tooth.

"Well, the only thing I know to do with something like this," said B.J., "is to take it to the Lord in prayer. He's bound to listen."

Over in the dogpen one of the German shepherds went for a Doberman, and the two dogs fought briefly, rolling and snapping in the dust for a minute or two.

"Yeah," said Barney Lee above the snarls and yips, "but what if you think your prayer ain't gonna carry no further than the top of this tent? What if you think nothing ain't tuned in to you?"

"Wait," said B.J., lifting his hand toward the back of the tent and holding his breath to listen. "I thought I heard some thunder." Both men got quiet, their heads turned toward the drawstring flap to listen, but all they could hear were the sounds of the dog fight trailing off. After a minute, even that stopped, and they sat hearing the sweat drip off Barney Lee's nose on to the groundcover.

"I guess it was just trucks on the highway," B.J. finally said in Barney Lee's direction. "Kneel down, Brother B. Lee, and let's talk to the Lord." B.J. rolled over onto his knees and kneeled with his back to the tent wall, taking a deep breath to begin and thinking as he did that Barney Lee was right: something in the mountaineer's tent did smell a little strange and sour.

41

Myrtle Shackleford's heart hurt. Right in the middle of her chest it sat like a boil, burning with fire at every beat and feeling as if it were going to pop wide open every time she took a breath, even the least one. She turned her head gently from one side to the other and knew by the crackling sounds deep in her skull that the wax in her ear canals was building up again to a bad level and was turning just as hard as rock as she sat there. One of the Cuban doctors at Coushatta County Memorial would have to take an instrument to both ears again, she just knew, and she groaned aloud at the thought of having to ride Van Ray Cox's bus all the way down there in the heat. And the doctor would be dark-haired and have a mustache, and he would jabber in Mexican to his nurse who would be a Mexican herself.

Myrtle didn't know what was worse, the waxy build-up in the tubes leading down into her head or the shooting pains, yellowish red in color, that ran up her back from her kidneys and gathered themselves into a big ball at the base of the back of her head right under where she had fastened her hair barrette. Maybe the worse thing of all was having to sit up so much to keep everything in the lower part of her body from running all over her system and seeping into every joint of her bones and getting stuck there in the little crevasses and chambers. She had to sleep each and every night propped up in bed, her back against a bolster to keep it contained low down somewhere, and sometimes by morning when the birds woke her up with their hollering, she could feel all of the lower body poisons rising up anyway, despite the discomfort she had suffered from sleeping sitting up.

When they had all night to rise in her body like sap going up in a sweet gum in the spring, the fluids and pains came to a kind

42

of container just under her breastbone, steadily filling and swelling until Myrtle had to belch out some vapors or die. She would do that, scratching the bedcovers with her fingers until she had two big wads of sheet in each hand and tilting her head back to make a smooth passage for the gas to come up through her throat and back out between her lips and through her nose. It would erupt with a savage barking sound, causing tears to pop out of her eyes and water to drip from her nostrils. "Jesus," she would say after each emission, "Sweet Blessed Savior, hold my hand in Thine."

Sitting there in the oak rocker in the living room, the only soul awake in the whole house though it was well after seven o'clock, Myrtle could sense deep in her bowels and in the back of her calves and thighs a coming pressure as the purple and green fluids began gathering themselves for the journey upward through the systems of her body. She groaned and made two weak fists on the arms of her rocker and listened for sounds from the other rooms of the house, but all she could hear were a couple of the German shepherds in the Christian Guard Dogs pen outside growling at each other.

She looked across at Burton's green sofa and comforted herself with the thought that if the coverlet thrown over it were lifted, she would be still able to see remnants of the shape of her second husband's body where it had forced itself into the cushions during the eight years it had spent lying there. She eased one foot off the floor a couple of inches, gently let it come back to rest again and lifted her eyes to the framed photograph hanging on the wall over the Dumont. It looked just like him, natural, even though he was wearing a suit and had his eyes closed, of course.

Ronnie Lee, one of Burton's nephews by his first wife, had stood on a chair at the end of his uncle's coffin, and he was tall anyway. So when he had taken the flash picture he had been well enough above everything to get a good angle. The shot looked about head-on. Little Sis had taken a pair of scissors to the snapshot and been able to cut away most of the coffin, and then she had put it into a frame behind some glass and turned the whole thing sideways and hung it on the wall. Lots of people who didn't know thought it was a picture of Burton Shackleford standing up in a kind of a relaxed pose in a nice blue suit. The only thing that didn't look right were the closed eyes, but as Bubba said about the picture of his father, he might have just blinked.

"Sweet Infant Child of God," Myrtle said, leaning her head back to clear a passage for the gas and lifting both feet off the floor in her struggle. "Lord, if it be Thy will." But the bubble hung back and refused the opening, and it wasn't until she heard the gravel in the driveway crunching under Bubba's pickup that Myrtle was able to coax it up. It came with a rush and a roar just as her younger son opened the front screen and stuck his head in.

"Howdy, Mama," he said. "Bilious this morning?"

"Bubba," she said, patting at her eyes and nose, "if you could only know the pain and pressure your mama has to suffer you would be crying like your heart was broken."

"I know, Mama, I know," Bubba said, coming into the room and flopping down on the green sofa. He was wearing a fresh suit of khakis that was beginning to wilt at the neck with sweat, and his eyes looked bloodshot even through his glasses.

"Did you wipe your feet, son?" Myrtle said, gesturing at the floor. "I'm trying to keep this house swept for B.J."

"Aw yeah, Mama. I ain't even been nowhere this morning yet to get my shoes dirty. I ain't even got a thing to do before this afternoon when I got to go out the Israel Road and unstop a toilet."

"Whose is it? Not some of the Murphys, is it?"

"No, it's some lady in a trailer house with a bad connection. One of them pipeline people out yonder, I reckon."

Myrtle nodded and looked at the green face of the Dumont. She could see in the morning sunlight that it needed dusting and that the crocheted doily on top of it was twisted off to one side.

"I can't get MayBelle to do nothing," she said to the Dumont.

"Uh huh," said Bubba. He leaned back on the sofa, loosened his belt a notch and then tilted his near shoulder toward his mother. "You know, of course, Mama, if you let the city hook this house and them three rent ones up I'm ruined. I might as well just give my pickup away and bust holes in all my holding tanks."

"Bubba," Myrtle said and then stopped for a minute to listen to her lower body. "It's gonna all be free, they say, and it would save me all the expense of upkeep from now on out." The green fluid whispered softly to the purple, and the purple answered back with a muted gurgle.

"That's what they say now, but you hook it on up and then blow out a flange or a coupling on down the road and see what the city says then."

Bubba took off his felt hat and punched a fist into the crown of it, collapsing it into a wad, and then remoulded it into its first shape. She never would do anything he asked her to, not when he was just a kid trying to keep up with B.J. and not now when the city was closing down septic tanks like it meant to outlaw them in the incorporated limits of Annette, Texas. B.J. got to go off to college and end up preaching in a big church on the Gulf coast, and what he ended up doing was installing galvanized shitcatchers in people's backyards. And now they were closing that door on him, and it was a science to the septic tank treatment of human waste, and his own mother was going over to the other side and taking all the houses on Sunflower Road with her.

"Your daddy was a forward-looking man, Bubba," Myrtle said. "I wished he was here to advise you."

"Yeah," said Bubba, twisting his neck so he couldn't see the picture of Burton standing up in the coffin, "he was forward-looking all right. He looked forward at that TV set yonder until he died of laziness, lying right here where I'm sitting."

"Your mother is a sick woman," Myrtle said around the clot of fumes gathering in her chest and throat. "I can barely sit here and listen to converse with you. Sometimes I just wish I had a little handle on the side of my neck that I could open and close."

Myrtle shifted in her seat from one side to the other, pushing with her right hand on the arm of the rocker and then pulling with it. "I don't even know if I'm going to be able to make it to the graveyard working this coming Sunday. Look at the veins in the back of my hand. They just pooch out at you." She held out her hand toward Bubba and let it quiver.

"Yeah, Mama," said Bubba, not looking at the hand, "that's what me and Little Sis have been worrying about. You don't get no real help living here, and you need to be somewhere you do." He stopped talking and looked over at his mother from under the brim of his hat. She was sitting braced with both hands on the rocker arms, feet dangling above the floor, her eyes focused on something four miles off. Encouraged, Bubba went on.

"See," he said, "you can't run everything around here no more with your health being what it is, and Aunt MayBelle is getting to where she don't even talk sense half the time. You got to get on out into a place where they'll take care of you. Me and Little Sis have been real concerned about your welfare."

Myrtle was only partially tuned in to Bubba's words. Half of her attention was being given to the reluctant pressure swelling in her upper body. "Come on up," she was saying under her breath, "come on up, bubble, now."

Little Sis was Avalene Shackleford, the only girl and the baby of the family. She had been valedictorian of her graduating class at Annette High School and had gone on to Drews Business College in Beaumont on the strength of the Shepherd's Laundry Tuition Scholarship. She had done real well there, earning A's in Typing and Stenography and Office Management and graduating with no trouble. The job of head secretary at Purvis Lumber Company in Goodrich had opened up just as Avalene finished school, and she had come back to Coushatta County to take it on, framed certificate in her eighty-word-per-minute hands.

For fourteen years she had lived in two rooms of an old lady's house in Goodrich with her cat Henry and come home to Annette almost every Saturday to see Mama. And on every Friday afternoon of the fourteen years, at the end of the week's work, Mr. Boyd Purvis, the owner of the lumber company, would lead her from behind her desk in the office to a little room in the back filled with paint cans and scrap lumber. Then he would lay her down on a surplus army cot and do all kinds of things to her until the quitting-time whistle sounded at the pulpwood sawmill out on the Goodrich highway. He missed only on holidays and the few times when one or the other of them had a cold or the flu.

Mr. Purvis had a sick wife he couldn't leave, he loved his children very deeply, and he was president of the Lion's Club. So that time between five-thirty and six o'clock on Fridays was all he could give Avalene from his life. The whole thing had made her bitter and nervous and caused her to drive her car at reckless speeds up and down Texas Highway 62. She already had a bridge abutment picked out just south of the Urbana cutoff, and she had promised herself that someday she would just point the nose of her Plymouth in the direction of the mass of gray cement and floorboard it.

"Sweet Jesus," said Myrtle, jolted by the bubble's sudden eruption, "stand by me, if it be Thy blessed will."

"You think about it now," Bubba was saying. "It's something we got to take care of quick. Me and Little Sis got it about worked out, and I know B.J.'s gonna agree with us."

Outside, an Annette City dump truck rumbled by in a cloud of dust, its bed filled with black men holding shovels ready to start digging somewhere on Sunflower Road. Bubba watched the red clay suspended in the dry air fan out to settle back to earth, and he coughed deeply in sympathy. Four septic tanks, he thought to himself, one right outside that window and three others at her rent houses, all of them in danger of stoppage. "It's my livelihood," he suddenly said out loud and jumped up from the sofa, headed for the rear of the house to find B.J. He had sweated through the back of his fresh khaki shirt.

II

Fire Ants

By the night of the second day MayBelle had managed to put a solid dent in the quart of clear communist whiskey. The level of the liquid stood just at the tip of the nose of the white Bear-King, a little less than one half of the way down the bottle. She had decided that she liked it better than any of the other kinds of liquor Van Ray Cox had left in the culvert on Sunflower Road for her before. After the first good mouthful, it didn't taste like much at all, and when she blew her breath into her hands and sniffed at it, all she could detect was a slight smell something like weak medicine or maybe the inside of an unwashed flower vase.

She had kept the bottle stuck down inside a basket of clothes that needed ironing, and throughout the course of the day whenever she had a chance to walk through the back room where the basket was kept, she would stop for the odd sip or two. By the middle of the afternoon, she had stopped feeling the heat even though she had cooked three coconut pies, one for B.J.'s supper and two for the graveyard working, and had ironed a dress for her and Myrtle. And by suppertime with Myrtle and B.J. and Bubba and Barney Lee Richards all around the table waiting for her to bring in the dishes from the kitchen, MayBelle had reached the point that she couldn't tell if she had put salt in the black-eyed peas or not, even when she tasted them twice, a whole spoonful each time.

"Aunt MayBelle," B.J. was saying, looking up at her with a big grin on his face, "where's that good cornbread? I bet old Barney Lee could eat some of that." He reached over and punched at one of Barney Lee's sides where it lapped over and hid his belt. "He looks hungry to me, this boy does."

"Aw, B.J.," said Barney Lee and hitched a little in his chair. "I shouldn't be eating at all, but I save up just enough to eat over here at your Mama's house."

"Well, you're always welcome," said Myrtle from the end of the table by the china cabinet. "We don't see enough of you around here. Used to, you boys were always underfoot. I wish it was that way now."

"Barney Lee," said MayBelle, and waited to hear what she was going to say, "your hair is going back real far on both sides of your head. Not as far as B.J.'s, but it's getting on back there all right." She moved over and set the pan of hot cornbread on a pad in the middle of the table. "You gonna be as bald as your old daddy in a few years."

MayBelle straightened up to go back to the kitchen for another dish, and the Bear-King winked at her and lifted a paw, making her not listen to what Myrtle was calling to her as she walked through the door of the dining room. Maybe I better go look at that clothes basket before I bring in that bowl of okra, she thought to herself, and made a little detour off the kitchen. The foreign bottle was safe where she had left it, and she adjusted the level of the vodka inside to where it came just to the white bear's neckline.

When she came back into the dining room with the okra, everybody was waiting for B.J. to say grace, sitting quiet at the table and cutting eyes at the pastor at the head of it. "Sit down for a minute, Aunt MayBelle," B.J. said in a composed voice and caught at her arm. "Let's thank the Lord and then you can finish serving the table."

MayBelle dropped into her chair and looked at a flower in the middle of the plate in front of her. It was pounding like a heart beating, and it did so in perfect time to the song of a mockingbird calling outside the window. It's the Texas State Bird, she thought, and Austin is the state capital. The native bluebonnet is the State Flower and grows wild along the highways every spring. But it's hard to transplant, and it smells just like a weed. If you got some on your hands, you can wash and wash them with heavy soap, and the smell will still be there for up to a week after. But they are pretty to look at, all the bluebonnets alongside the highway. There were big banks of them on both sides of the dirt road for as far as you could see, and when the car went by them it made enough wind to show the undersides of the flowers, lighter blue than the tops of the petals.

He stopped the car so they could look at all of them on both sides of the road, and a little breeze came up just when he turned the engine off, and it went across the bluebonnets like a wave. It was like ripples in a pond, they all turned together in rings and the light blue traveled along the tops of the darker blue petals as if it wasn't just the west wind moving things around, but something else all by itself.

He asked her if she didn't think it was the prettiest thing she ever saw, and she said yes and turned in the seat to face him.

And that's when he reached out his hand and put it on the back of her head and said her eyes put him in mind of the color on the underside of the bluebonnets, and he had always wanted to tell her that. It was hot, early May, and there was a little line of sweat on his upper lip and when he came toward her she watched that until her eyes couldn't focus on it anymore he was so close and then his mouth was on hers and it was open and there was a little smell of cigarette smoke.

She could hear the hot metal of the car ticking in the sun, it was hers, the only one she ever owned and that was only for a little over a year. It set high off the road and could go over deep ruts and not get stuck and it could climb any hill in Coushatta County without having to shift gears. The breeze was coming in the car window off the bluebonnets and it felt cool, but his hands were hot wherever they touched her and she kept her eyes closed and could still see the light blue underside of the flowers and the thin line of sweat on his lip and she was ticking all over just like the new car sitting still between the banks of bluebonnets in the sun.

"All this we ask in Thy Name, Amen," said B.J. and reached for the plate of cornbread. "You can go get the mashed potatoes now, Aunt MayBelle."

"Yes," said Myrtle, looking across the table at her, "and another thing too while you're in the kitchen. You poured me sweet milk in my glass, and you know I've got to have clabbermilk at supper."

Everybody allowed as how the vegetables were real good for this late in the season, but that the blackberry cobbler was a little tart. It was probably because of the dry spell, Barney Lee said, and they all agreed that the wild berries had been hard hit this year and might not even make at all next summer unless they got some relief.

After supper Myrtle and Barney Lee went into the living room to catch the evening news on the Dumont, and B.J. put on his quilted suit and went out with Bubba and the cattle prod to agitate the Dobermans and German shepherds.

From where she stood by the sinkful of dishes, MayBelle could hear the dogs begin barking and growling as soon as they saw B.J. and Bubba coming toward the pen. She ran some more water into the sink, hot enough to turn her hands red when she reached into it, and she almost let it overflow before she turned off the faucet and started washing. She didn't break but one dish, the flowered plate off which she had eaten a little okra and a few crowder peas at supper, but dropping it didn't seem to help the way she felt any.

She stood looking down at the parts it had cracked into on the floor, feeling the heat from the soapy water rising into her chest and face and hearing the TV set booming two rooms away, and decided she would look into the clothes basket again as soon as she had finished in the kitchen.

Outside a dog yipped and Bubba laughed, and MayBelle lifted her eyes to the window over the sink. The back pasture was catching the last rays of the setting sun, and it looked almost gold in the light. But when she looked closer, she could see that the yellow color was in the weeds and sawgrass itself, not just borrowed from the sun, and what looked like haze was really the dry seed pods rattling at the ends of the stalks.

Further up the hill yellowish smoke was rising from one of the cabins in the quarter, perfectly straight up into the sky as far as she could see, not a waver or a bit of motion to it. She stood watching it for a long time, dishcloth in one hand and a soapy glass in the other, until finally her eye was caught by a small figure moving slowly across the back edge of the pasture and disappearing into the dark line of pines that enclosed it.

That's old Sully, she said to herself, probably picking up kindling or looking at a rabbit trap. Wonder how he stands the heat of a wood cookstove this time of the year. Keeps it going all the time, too, Cora says.

In the living room Barney Lee asked Myrtle something, and she answered him, not loud enough to be understood, and MayBelle went back to the dishwashing, rinsing and setting aside the glass she was holding. It had a wide striped design on it, and it felt right in her hand as she sat it on the drainboard to dry.

Picking up speed, she finished the rest of the glassware, the knives and forks, the cooking pots and the cornbread skillet, and then wiped the counters dry and swabbed off the top of the gas stove. By the time she finished turning the coffee pot upside down on the counter next to the sink, the striped glass on the drainboard had dried and a new program had started on the television set. The sounds of a happy bunch of people laughing and clapping their hands came from the front part of the house as MayBelle picked up her glass and walked out of the kitchen toward the backroom.

She filled the glass up to the top of where the colored stripe began and took two small sips of the clear bitter liquid. She stopped, held the foreign bottle up to the light and watched the Bear-King while she drained the rest of the glass in one long swallow. A little of the vodka got up her nose, and she almost sneezed but managed to hold it back, belching deeply to keep things balanced. As she did, the Bear-King nodded his head, causing a sparkle of light to flash from his crown, and lifted one paw a fraction. "Thank you, Mr. Communist," MayBelle said, "I believe I will."

A few minutes later, Bubba Shackleford looked up from helping B.J. untangle one of the German shepherds which had got a front foot hung in the wire noose on the end of the cattle prod, barely avoiding getting a hand slashed as he did, and caught sight of something moving down the hill in the back pasture. But by the time he got around to looking again, after getting the dog loose and back in the pen and the gate slammed shut, whatever it was had got too far off to see through his sweated-up glasses.

"B.J.," he said and waved toward the back of the house, "was that Aunt MayBelle yonder in the pasture?"

"Where?" said B.J. through the Johnny Bench mask in a cross voice. He laid the electric prod down in the dust of the yard and pulled the suit away from his neck so he could blow down his collar. He felt hot enough in the outfit to faint, and the dust kicked up by the last dog had got all up in his facemask, mixing with the sweat and leaving muddy tracks at the corners of his cheeks.

"What would she be doing in that weedpatch? She's in the house last I notice."

"Aw, nothing," said Bubba. "If it was her, she just checking out the blackberries, I reckon. It don't make no difference."

"Bubba," said B.J. and paused to get his breath and look at the pen of barking dogs in front of him. "I believe Christian Guard Dogs, Incorporated has made some real progress in the last few days. Look at them fighting and snapping in there. Why, they'd tear a prowler all to pieces in less than two minutes."

"B.J.," Bubba answered. "Watch this." He picked up the dead pine limb and rattled the hogwire with it, and immediately the nearest Doberman lunged at the fence, snapping and foaming at the steel wire between its teeth, its eyes narrow and bloodshot.

"That dog there," Bubba announced in a serious flat voice, "would kill a stray nigger or a doped-up hippie in a New York minute."

"I figure you got to do what you can," said B.J., "and if there's a little honest profit in it for a Christian, it's nothing wrong with that." B.J. took off the catcher's mask and stood for a minute watching the worked-up dogs prowl up and down the pen, baring their teeth at each other as they passed, their tails carried low between their legs and the hair on their backs all roughed up. Then he turned toward his brother and clapped him on the shoulder.

"Let's go get a drink of water and talk about your business problems, Bubba. The Lord'll find an answer for you. You just got to give Him a chance."

The houses were lined up on each side of a dirt road that came up from the patch of weeds to the south and stopped abruptly at the edge of the pasture. In front of the first one on the left, a cabin with two front doors opening into the same room and a window in between them with a pane of unbroken glass still in it, was the body of a '54 Chevrolet up on blocks. All four wheels had been taken off a long time ago and fastened together with a length of log chain and hung from the lowest limb of an oak tree. The bark on the oak had grown over and around the chain, and the metal of the wheels had fused together with rust.

MayBelle took another sip straight from the bottle and stepped around a marooned two-wheeled tricycle, grown up in bitterweeds, careful not to trip herself up. She walked up on the porch of the next shotgun house and leaned over to peer through a knocked-out window. Her footsteps on the floorboards sounded like a drum, she noticed, and she hopped up and down a couple of times to hear the low boom again. There was enough vodka left in the bottle to slosh around as she did so, and she shook it in her right hand until it foamed. It didn't seem to bother the Bear-King any.

The only thing left in the front room was a two-legged wood stove tilted over to one side and three walls covered with pictures of movie stars, politicians and baseball players. "Howdy, Mr. and Mrs. President," MayBelle said to a large photograph of JFK and Jackie next to a picture of Willie Mays and just below one of Bob Hope. "How y'all this evening?" She took another little sip and had a hard time getting the top screwed back on, and by the time she had it down tight, it was getting too difficult in the fading light to distinguish one face on the wall from another, so she quit trying.

The back of the next cabin had been completely torn off, so when MayBelle stepped up on the porch and looked through the door all she could see was a framed scene of the dark woods behind. A whip-poor-will called from somewhere deep inside the picture, and after a minute was answered by another one further off. MayBelle held her breath to listen, but neither bird made another sound, and after a time, she stepped back down to the road and looked at the clear space around her.

She felt as though it was getting dark too quickly and she hadn't been able to see all she wanted. Already the tops of the bank of pines around the row of houses were vanishing into the sky, and one by one the features of everything around her, the stones in the road and the discarded jars and tin cans, the bits and pieces of old automobiles, the broken furniture lying around the porches and the shiny things tacked up on the wall and around the edges of the eaves, were slipping away as the light steadily diminished. Whatever it was she had come to see, she hadn't discovered yet, and she shivered a little, hot as it was, feeling the need to move on until she found it. I waited too late in the day again, she thought, and now I can't see anything.

It was like the time at Holly Springs she had been playing in the loft of the barn with some of the Stutts girls and had slipped down between the beams and the shingles of the roof to hide. Papa had found her there at supper time, passed out from the sting of wasps whose nest she had laid her head against, her face covered with bumps and her eyes swollen shut from the poison. He had carried her down to Double Pen Creek, the coldest water in the county, running with her in his arms two miles through the cotton fields and the second-growth thickets until he was able to lay her in the water and draw off the fire of the wasp stings. She hadn't been able to see for six days after that, even after the swelling went down and she was able to open her eyes finally. The feeling of the light fading and the dark creeping up came on her again as she stood in the road between the rows of ruined houses, the bottle from the culvert tight in her hand.

"You looking for Cora, her place down yonder."

MayBelle lifted her gaze from the Bear-King and focused in the direction from where the voice had come. In a few seconds she picked him out of the shadow at the base of a sycamore trunk two houses down. He was a little black man in a long coat that dragged the ground and his hair was as white as cotton.

"You Sully," declared MayBelle and took a drink from her quart bottle.

"Yes, ma'am," said the little black man and giggled high up through his nose. "That be me. Old Sully."

"You used to do a little work for Burton Shackleford. Down yonder." She waved the bottle off to the side without looking away from the sycamore shadow.

"That's right," he called out in a high voice to the empty houses, looking from one side of the open space to the other and then taking a couple of steps out into the road. "You talking about me, all right. I shore used to do a little work for Mister Burton. Build some fence. Dig them foundations. Pick up pecans oncet in a while."

"Uh huh," said MayBelle and paused for a minute. Two whip-poor-wills behind the backless house traded calls again, further away this time than before.

"I heard a lot about you. Cora she told me."

"Say she did," said Sully and kicked at something in the dust of the road. "Cora you say?"

"That's right," MayBelle said, addressing herself to the Bear-King and lifting the bottle to her mouth. The liquor had stopped tasting good a while back and now seemed like nothing more than water.

"She says," MayBelle said and paused to pat at her lips with the tips of her fingers, "Cora says you're still a creeper."

"She say that?" Sully asked in an amazed voice and scratched at the cotton on top of his head. "That's a mystery to me. She uh old woman. Last old woman in the quarter." He stopped and looked off at the tree line, then down at whatever he had kicked at in the sand and finally at the bottle in MayBelle's hand.

"What that is?" he said. MayBelle raised the bottle to eye-level and shook its contents back and forth against the Bear-King's feet, "That there liquor is communist whiskey."

Then both regarded the bottle for a minute without saying anything as the liquid moved from one side to the other more and more slowly until it finally settled to dead level in MayBelle's steady grasp.

"Say it is?" Sully finally said after a while.

"Uh huh. You ever drink any of this communist whiskey?"

"No ma'am, Miz MayBelle. I uh Baptist," Sully said. "If I's to vote, I vote that straight Democrat ticket."

MayBelle unscrewed the lid, took a hard look at the level of the side of the bottle, and then carefully sipped until she had brought the liquid down to where the Bear-King appeared to be barely walking on the water beneath his feet.

"You don't drink nothing then," she said to Sully, carefully replacing the metal cap and giving it a pat.

"Nothing communist, no ma'am, but I do like to sip a little of that white liquor that Rufus boy bring me now and again. Some body over yonder in Leggett or Marston they makes that stuff."

"Is it hot?"

"Is it hot," declared Sully. "Sometimes I gots to sit down to drink from that Mason jar."

"Tell you what, Sully," said MayBelle and gave the little

black man a long look over the neck of the bottle.

"Yes, ma'am," he said and straightened to attention until just the edges of his coat were touching the dust of the road. "What's that?"

"You go get yourself a clean glass and bring me one too, and I'll let you have a taste of this communist whiskey." Sully spun around to leave and she called after him: "You got any of that Mason jar bring it on too."

"It be here directly," Sully answered over his shoulder and hopped over a discarded table leg in his way.

MayBelle walked over to the nearest porch and sat down to wait, her feet stuck straight out in front of her, and began trying to imitate the whip-poor-will's call, sending her voice forth into the darkness in a low quavering tone, but not a bird had answered, no matter how she listened, by the time Sully got back with two jelly glasses and a Mason jar full of yellow shine, the sheen and consistency of light oil.

"You gone fell down again in amongst all the weeds, Miz MayBelle," Sully said, "you keep on trying to skip."

"I have always loved to skip," said MayBelle, moving through the pasture down the hill at a pretty good clip. She caught one foot on something in the dark and stepped high with the other one, bobbing to one side like a boxer in the ring.

"Watch me now," she said. "Yessir. Goddamn."

"You show do cuss a lot for a white lady," said Sully, dodging and weaving through the rank saw grass and bull-nettles.

"I know it. Damn. Hell. Shit-fart."

"Uh huh," said Sully, hurrying to catch up and trying to see how far they had reached in the Shackleford back pasture. The moon was down, and he was having a hard time judging the distance to the stile over the back fence, what with his coat catching on weeds and sticks and the yellow shine thundering in his head.

He bent down to free his hem from something that had snagged it, felt the burn of bullnettle across his hand, and recognized a clump of trees against the line of the night sky.

"I'se you," he called ahead in a high whisper. "I'd keep to the left right around here. Them old fire ants's bed just over yonder."

"Where?" said MayBelle, stopping in the middle of a skip so abruptly that she slipped on something which turned under her foot and almost caused her to fall. "Where are them little boogers?"

"Just over yonder about fifteen, twenty feet," Sully said, glad to stop and take a deep breath to settle the moving shapes around him. "See where them weeds stick up, look like a old cowboy's hat? Them ants got they old dirt nest just this side." He paused to smooth his coat around him and rub his bullnettle burn. "That there where they sleep when they ain't out killing things."

"You say they tough," said the skinny white lady. "It burns when they bite?"

"Burns? Lawdy have mercy. Do it burn when they bites? Everywhere one of them fire ants sting you it's a little piece of your hide swell up and rot out all around it. Take about a week to happen."

Sully felt the ground begin to tilt to one side, and he lifted one foot and brought it down sharply to level things out. The earth pushed back hard, but by keeping his knee locked, he was able to hold it steady. "I don't know how long I can last," he said to his right leg, "but I do what I can."

"Shit, goddamn," said MayBelle, "let's go see if they're all asleep in their bed."

"You mean them fire ants? They kill the baby birds and little rabbits in they nestes. Chop 'em up, take'm home and eat'm. I don't want no part of them boogers. I ain't lost nothing in them fire ants' bed."

"Well, I believe I did," said MayBelle. "Piss damn. I'm gonna go over there and go to bed with them."

Sully heard the dry weeds crack and pop as the white lady began moving toward the cowboy hat shape, and he lifted his foot to step toward the sound. When he did, the released earth flew up and hit him all down the right side of his body and against his ear and jaw. "I knowed it was going to happen," he said to his right leg as he lay, half stunned in the high weeds, "I let things go too quick."

By the time he was able to get up again, scrambling to find one knee, then the other, and then flapping his arms about him to get all the way off the ground and away from its terrible grip, the skinny white lady had already reached the fire ant bed and dropped down beside it. Sully moved at an angle, one arm much higher than the other and his ears ringing with the lick the ground had just given him, until he came up close enough to see the dark bulk of the old woman stretched out in the soft mound of ant-chewed earth.

"You got to get up from there, Miz MayBelle," he said and began to lean toward her, hand outstretched, but then thought better of it as he felt the earth begin to gather itself for another go at him.

She was speaking in a crooning voice to the ant bed, saying words he couldn't understand and moving herself slowly from side to side as she settled into it.

"Miz MayBelle," Sully said, "crawl on up out of there now. They gonna eat you alive lying there. That ain't no fun."

"Don't you put a hand on me, Papa," she said in a clear hard voice, suddenly getting still, "I'm right where I want to be."

"I see I got it to do," Sully said and threw his head back to look around for somebody. He couldn't see a soul, and every star in the night sky was perfectly clear and still.

"You decide to get up while I'm gone," he said to the dark shape at his feet, "just go on ahead and do it."

Running in a half-crouch with one arm out for balance against the tilt the earth was putting on him, Sully started down the hill toward the back fence of the Shackleford place, proceeding through the weeds and brambles like a sailboat tacking into the wind. About every fifty feet, he had to lean into a new angle and cut back to keep the ground from reaching up and slamming him another lick, and the dirt of the dry field and the hard edges of the saw grass were working together like a charm to slow and trip him up.

He went over the stile on his hands and knees, and the earth popped him a good one again on the other side of the fence, but he was able to get himself up by leaning his back against the trunk of a pine tree and pushing himself up in stages. There was a dim yellow light coming from a cloth tent right at the back steps of the house, and Sully aimed for that and the sounds of a man's voice coming from it in a regular singing pattern. He got there in three more angled runs, the last one involving a low clothesline that caught him in the head just where his hairline started, and he stopped about ten feet from the tent flap, dust rising around him and the earth pushing up hard against one foot and sucking down at the other one.

Barney Lee Richards lifted the tent flap and stuck his head out to see what had caused all the commotion in the middle of B.J.'s prayer against the unpardonable sin, but at first all he could make out was a cloud of suspended dust with a large dark shape in the middle of it. He blinked his eyes, focused again, and the form began to resolve itself into somebody or something standing at an angle, an arm extended above its head, which looked whiter than anything around it, and the whole thing wrapped in a long hanging garment. The clothesline was making a strange humming sound.

"Aw naw," he said in a choked disbelieving voice, jerked his head back inside the lighted tent, and spun around to look at B.J., his eyes opened wide enough to show white all around them.

"B.J.," he said, "it's something all black wearing an old long cape and it's got white on its head and it's pointing its hand up at the sky."

"At the sky?" said B.J. and began to fumble around in the darkness of the tent floor with both hands for his Bible. "You say it's wearing a long cape?"

"That's right, that's right," said Barney Lee in a high whine and began to cry. He heaved himself forward onto his hands and knees and lurched into a rapid crawl as if he were planning to tear out the back of the mountaineer's tent, colliding with B.J. and causing him to lose his grip on the Bible he had just found next to a paper sack full of bananas.

"Hold still, Barney Lee," B.J. said. "Stop it now. I'm trying to get hold of something to help us if you'll just set still and let me."

To Sully on the outside, standing breathless and stunned next to the clothesline pole, the commotion in the two-man tent made it look as though the shelter was full of a small pack of hounds fighting over a possum. First one wall, then the other bulged and stretched, and the ropes fastened to the tent stakes groaned and popped under the pressure. The stakes themselves seemed to shift and glow in the dark as he watched.

"White folks," Sully said in a weak voice and then, getting a good breath, "white folks. I gots to talk to you."

The canvas of the tent suddenly stopped surging, and everything became quiet. Sully stood tilted to one side and braced against the pull of the earth, his mouth half-open to listen, but all he could hear for fully a minute was the sound of the yellow shine seeping and sliding through his head and from far off somewhere in the woods the call of a roosting bird that had waked up in the night.

Finally the front flap of the tent opened up a few inches and the bulk of a man's head appeared in the crack.

"Who's that out there?" the head asked.

"Hidy, white folks," said Sully. "It's only just me. Old Sully. Just only an ordinary old field nigger. Done retire."

The flap moved all the way open, and B.J. crawled halfway out the tent, straining to get a better look.

"It's just an old colored gentleman, Brother B. Lee," he said over his shoulder. "Like I told you, it ain't nothing to worry about."

"Well," said Barney Lee from the darkness behind him, "I was afraid it was something spiritual. Why was it standing that way with its hand pointing up, if it was a nigger?"

"Hello, old man," said B.J., all the way out of the tent now and standing up to brush the dirt off his pants. "Kinda late at night to be calling, idn't it?"

"Yessir," said Sully. "It do be late, but a old man he don't sleep much. He don't need what he use to."

"Uh huh," B.J. said and turned back to help Barney Lee who had climbed halfway up but had gotten stuck with one knee bent and the other leg fully extended.

"Why," Barney Lee addressed the man in the long coat, "Why you standing that way with your arm sticking way up like that?"

"Well sir," said Sully and turned his head to look up along his sleeve. "It seem like it help me to stand like this." The shine made a ripple in a new little path in his head, and he had to lift his hand higher to keep things whole and steady.

"I just wish you'd listen to that, Barney Lee," B.J. said in a tight voice.

"What? I don't hear nothing."

"That's exactly what I'm talking about. Here's this old nig-colored gentleman—come walking up in the dead of night, and what do you hear from them dogs? Not a thing."

Everybody stopped to listen and had to agree that the dog pen was showing no sign of alert.

"And I thought the training was going along so good the last few days. I'm getting real discouraged about Christian Guard Dogs." B.J. sighed deeply, kicked at the ground, and coughed at the dust hanging in the air. "I don't know. I just don't know."

"However," said Sully, "what it is I come up here and bother you white folks about it be up yonder in the pasture." He swung a hand back in the direction he had come, almost lost the hold he was maintaining against the steady pull of the earth, and staggered a step or two before he found it again.

"Say it helps you to stand like that?" asked Barney Lee and shyly stuck one arm above his head until it pointed in the direction of the Little Dipper. "Reckon it helps circulation or something?"

"Didn't make one peep," said B.J. "I didn't hear bark one, much less a growl."

"Yessir, white folks, it up yonder in the pasture. What I come here to your pulp tent for." Sully's arm was getting heavy so he ventured to lean against the pole supporting the clothesline and found that helped him some. Things were tilted, but not moving.

"A few minute ago, I was outside my house walking to that patch of cane. You know, tending to my business and that's when I heard her yonder."

"Who?" said B.J., making conversation as he looked over at the dark outline of the Christian Guard Dog pen as though he could see each individual Doberman and shepherd.

"Miz MayBelle."

"MayBelle? Aunt MayBelle Holt?" B.J. turned back to look at the little black man leaned up against the pole. "You say you heard her up in the nigger quarters?"

"Naw sir, white folks, not rightly in the quarters. She in that back pasture lying down in that fire ant bed."

"The fire ant bed?"

"Yessir, old Sully was in the quarters and she in the bed of fire ants."

"What's Aunt MayBelle doing in the fire ant bed? Did she fall into there?"

"I don't know about that," said Sully and adjusted his pointing arm more precisely with relation to the night sky. "I only just seed her in there a talking to them boosters."

"Come on, Brother B. Lee," B.J. said and broke into a trot toward the back fence. "We got to see what's going on. Them things will eat her up."

"That' as just the very thing I thought," said Sully, lurching away from the clothesline pole, and stumbling into a run after B.J., his gesturing right arm the only thing keeping him away from another solid lick from the ground. "I thought it sure wasn't no good idea for a white lady to lie down in amongst all them biting things."

"I'm coming, B.J.," called Barney Lee, a few steps behind Sully but close enough that the old man's flapping coat-tail sent puffs of dust up into his face. As he ran through the fence at the bottom of the hill, he raised an arm above his head and immediately felt his wind get better and his speed increase a step or two.

"I believe," Barney Lee said between breaths to the tilted sidling figure moving ahead of him, "that it's doing me good too. Pointing my arm up at the sky like this."

"Yessir, white folks," Sully said to the words coming from behind him, fighting as best he could against the yearn of the earth beneath his feet. It was going to get him at the stile again, he knew, but he had to live with that fact. "I just get them fat white folks to the ant bed, I quit," he said to the clouds of dust floating up before him. "You can have all of it then. I give it on up." He ran on, changing to a new tack every few feet, the pointing arm dead in the air above him, and listened to the shine rumble and slide through all the crannies of his head.

"It's gonna be hard times in the morning," he said out loud and aimed at the fence stile coming up. "It most always is."

You've got to say something to me, she said. You don't talk to me right. Now you got to say something to me.

I'm talking to you, he said. I'm talking right now to you. What you want me to say? This?

And he did a thing that made her eyes close and the itching start in her feet and begin to move up the back of her legs and across her belly and along her sides down each rib. Oh, she said, it's all in my shoulders and the back of my neck.

She let him push her further back until her head touched the green and gold bedspread, and one of her hands slipped off his shoulder and fell beside her as though she had lost all the strength in that part of her body. The arm was numb, but tingling like it did in the morning sometimes when she had slept wrong on it and cut off the circulation of blood. She tried to lift it and something like warm air ran up and down the inside of her upper arm and settled in her armpit under the bunched-up sleeve of the dress.

No, she said, it's hot and I'm sweating. It's going to get all over her bed. It'll make a wet mark, and it won't dry and she'll see it.

He said no and mumbled something else into the side of her throat that she couldn't hear. Something was happening to the bottoms of her feet and the palms of her hands. It was crawling and picking lightly at the skin. Just pulling it up a little at a time and letting it fall back and doing it over again until it felt like little hairs were raising up in their places and settling back over and over.

Talk to me, she said into his mouth. Say some things to me. You never have said a thing yet to me.

I'll say something to you, he said, and moved against her in a way that caused her to want to try to touch each corner of the bed.

If I put one foot at the edge down there and the other one at the other corner and then my hands way out until I can touch where the mattress comes to a point, then if some body was way up above us and could look down just at me and the way I'm laying here, it would look like two straight lines crossing in the middle. That makes an X when two lines cross. And in the middle where they cross is where I am.

Please, she said to the little burning spots that were beginning to start at each end of the leg of the X and to move slowly towards the intersection, come reach each other. Meet in the middle where I am.

But the little points of fire, like sparks that popped out of the fireplace and made burn marks on the floor, were taking their own time, stopping at one place for a while and settling there as if they were going to stay and not go any further and then when something finally burned through and broke apart, moving up a little further to settle a space closer to the middle of the X.

Just a word or two, she said to him, that's all I want you to say.

He said something back to her, something deep in his throat, but her ears were listening to a dim buzz that had started up deep inside her head, and she couldn't hear him.

What? she said. What? One foot and one hand had reached almost to the opposite corners of the bed and she strained, trying to make that line of the X straight and true before she turned her mind to the other line.

He moved above her, and suddenly the first line fell into place and locked itself, and the little burning spots along that whole leg of the X began to gather themselves and move more quickly from each end toward the middle where they might meet.

The buzz inside her head that wouldn't let her hear suddenly stopped the way you would click off a radio, and the sound of a mockingbird's call somewhere outside came twice and acted like something being poured into her head. It moved down inside like water and made two little points of pressure which were the bird calls and which stayed, waiting for something.

You talk to her, she said to him, her mouth so close to the side of his head when she spoke that her lips moved against the short hairs growing just behind his ear. I hear you say things to her. In the night. I hear you in the night. Lots of times.

Her other foot and hand were moving now on their own, and she no longer had to tell them what to do. The fingers of the hand reached, stretched, fell short, tried again and touched the edges of the mattress where the two sides came together. The green and gold spread moved in a fold beneath the hand, and as it did, the foot which formed the last point of the two legs of the X finally found its true position, and the intersecting lines fell into place at last, straight as though they had been drawn by a ruler. And whoever was looking at her from above could see it, the two legs of the X drawing to a point in the middle where they crossed and touched, and something let the burning points know the straight path was clear, and they came with a rush from each far point of the two lines, racing to meet in the middle where everything came together.

Say it, she managed to get the words out just before all of it reached the middle which was where she was, and he said something, but she couldn't hear anything but the fixed cry of the mockingbird and she blended her voice with that, and all the burning points came together and touched and flared and stayed.

"These sting is from insect, you say?" asked the Cuban doctor and probed with a plastic stick at the sprinkling of red welts running along the underside of MayBelle's right arm.

"That's right, doctor er-ah," said B.J. as the dark-skinned man inspected the other arm and then looked under the white sheet covering MayBelle from head to toe.

"Alesandro," he said and bowed over to look at MayBelle's throat.

"What's that?"

"My name. Is Alesandro," the doctor said and straightened up.

"Uh huh," said B.J. and looked over at Barney Lee who was standing next to a white cabinet with his arm stuck up in the air. He lowered it a few inches when he saw B.J. looking at him but not past shoulder level. The arm was getting heavy with fatigue, but it seemed to be a trade-off with his problem with getting his breath. He figured it was worth getting used to.

"Is it going to rot out all around them bites?" said B.J. to the Cuban.

"No," said Doctor Alesandro in his little foreigner's voice. "I give her cortisone shot. It go down the swelling. She use salve on externals it be well soon."

"She ain't in no danger then?" said Barney Lee from his spot by the metal cabinet of the Coushatta County Emergency Room.

"No, she's old woman but strong. It's good thing she's drunk though."

"Drunk?" said B.J. and Barney Lee in one voice.

"Yes. It slow the poison down so her heart is not—what is the English?—effect?"

"Listen here, Doctor Alex," said B.J., getting up from the metal stool he was sitting on. "Aunt MayBelle couldn't be drunk. Why, she's a fine Baptist lady."

"It's in the blood," said the Cuban. "One thing I tell you about the blood. She don't lie. It's the same in Texas as in Cuba. It's something to believe in." He motioned B.J. and Barney toward the door and pushed a buzzer in the wall.

"She stay tonight in hospital. Leave tomorrow afternoon probably. You go now. I must sew up the razor cut in the face of a Negro hombre now."

"Well," said Barney Lee out in the hall as he trotted along behind B.J. trying to keep up while he held his arm above his head. "Where do you suppose she got the whiskey now?"

"I didn't smell any whiskey, Brother B. Lee," said B.J. "I don't care what that little greaser said. My sweet old aunt ain't drunk." He stopped to open the glass and metal door for Barney Lee and followed him out into the hospital parking lot.

"I believe," he said bitterly as he got into the Oldsmobile and fired it up, " that that doctor is some kind of a communist."

"I hear they all hung real heavy," said Barney Lee.

III

Hunt

"**T**hat one yonder is the head dog then?" said B.J., looking at the black and tan hound curled up in the dust by one of the sections of oak stump supporting the front porch of the house. It was getting on toward evening, and the long shadows of the afternoon sun fell across all of the dog but his head and part of one front leg.

"Yeah," said Uncle Font Nowlen, "he ain't gonna lie to you on trail."

As they watched, the sun-lit leg kept up a steady pawing motion at the red dust beneath it, maintaining a regular measured beat as though it were moving in time to some song that only the dog could hear.

"Why's he scratching like that?" said one of the other men

standing in Uncle Font's front yard. "Is he killing fleas?" The man was called Mr. Hall, he was up on the weekend from Beaumont for one of Uncle Font Nowlen's cat hunts, and he was wearing brand new clothes of a camouflage design: boots, trousers, jacket and hat. The jacket had zippers, pockets and openings arranged in symmetrical patterns all over it. Each piece of metal on the clothing was tinted dull gray to avoid giving any kind of reflection. Mr. Hall's boots had left perfect impressions of their tread wherever he had stepped in the skinned-off yard in front of Uncle Font's double-log house.

"Naw," said Uncle Font and leaned over to spit a big wad of Cotton Boll tobacco juice into the center of one of the boot-tracks Mr. Hall had made. "He ain't scratching no fleas. Nor ticks neither."

He rolled the cud of tobacco from one cheek to the other and looked over at the black and tan.

"Name's Elvis," he said. "I'll show you why."

At the sound of the words the hound flopped his tail in the dust once and looked up at Uncle Font from under the ridges of tan markings over his eyes. He took a deep breath, expelled it with a sigh and advanced three steps away from his spot under the edge of the porch, ending up standing about eight or ten feet in front of and facing Uncle Font. Although the dog had come to a standstill, the front half of his body continued to bob up and down at a rhythmical pace, first to the left and then the right, his forelegs flexing and working, now and then one foot or the other leaving the ground briefly to paw gently at the dusty yard.

"Why, I swear he looks like he's dancing," said Mr. Hall's friend in a Gulf coast voice.

"Can't help but do it," Uncle Font said. "He's jitterbugging. That's why he's named what he is. Elvis."

The circle of cat hunters watched for a while without saying anything, until finally Elvis sat back on his haunches to scratch at an ear. Even during this operation, though, he kept up a steady movement, holding to his established rhythm and not missing a beat.

"How'd you teach him that?" asked Mr. Hall, fumbling at one of the zippers in his jacket.

"Didn't," said Uncle Font. "Distemper when he was a pup left him with that movement. It's a natural dance, that thing is. You can't learn a dog nor a human being neither to do nothing like that. You got to be give something like that. Just like Elvis Presley had a natural gift."

Uncle Font spit again and then lifted a carved cow horn hung around his neck with a rawhide string to his lips and blew two notes on it. Elvis got to all four feet and increased the tempo of his beat by about a quarter, and three other spotted dogs came surging into the front yard from under the house, two yipping in high voices and one baying in a low mournful tone.

"That blue tick there," B.J. said to Mr. Hall, pointing to the last dog out from under the porch, "him with that low voice, you know what Uncle Font calls him?"

"No," said Mr. Hall. "This is my first time to hunt up here with the old gentleman. Isn't he a character?" He smiled and pulled a hand away from one zipper on his jacket and made for another. "What is that speckled one named?"

"Johnny Cash," said B.J. "He talks so low on trail. The other one there is Johnny Ray because he sounds like he's crying when he's got something treed. And that one yonder, well..." B.J. paused and studied the fourth dog in the pack, a small blue tick with one ear gone and long scars running all the way from the tip of its nose halfway down its back. "Uncle Font calls him a curse word which I can't repeat. I'm a Baptist minister, you understand."

"Why me and my wife are members of First Baptist in Port Neches," said Mr. Hall and stuck out his hand. "Pleased to be hunting with you, Reverend."

"Just call me B.J.," said B.J. "I'm just one of the boys when

I get out in the woods."

"I hope you don't mind us taking a drink now and then tonight, preacher," said the other man, overhearing.

"No, no," B.J. answered him, looking over at the little man who seemed to have a basketball badly hidden under the front of his red plaid shirt. "It's not for me to judge the weakness of other folks."

"You fellers," called Uncle Font from over by Mr. Hall's pickup truck/house trailer combination, "we got to get into the woods."

The vehicle was a Nomad Home-on-Wheels, and as Mr. Hall watched, Uncle Font spit a load onto the rear hubcap and opened the door to the housing compartment for the dogs. The hounds swarmed the little set of steps that had flopped down as the door opened, Elvis jiving in the lead, and surged aboard in one big clot of black and tan and blue-tick spots, giving voice all the way in.

"I believe that's the first time they ever been in a house afore," said Uncle Font and clicked the door shut, the pickup rocking back and forth on its springs as the pack tumbled from one side to the other of the living compartment. "I was kinda afraid Goddam Son-of-a-Bitch wouldn't take to a place with beds and a stove in it."

"That's the name of the other blue-tick," B.J. said to Mr. Hall who stood with the corners of his mouth turned down and his eyes popped, watching the dogs fighting to get their muzzles up against each window in turn in the Nomad camper.

"You ain't got nothing in that little room to ruin their noses, have you?" Uncle Font asked Mr. Hall.

"No, I..."

"Cause if you have they ain't gonna be able to scent no bobcat." He paused to shift his cud of Cotton Boll and spit. "Hell, they couldn't smell skunk piss if you got something like loose cigarettes to eat or a opened sardine can for them to get into in yonder."

"No, I don't think so. I hope the dogs won't..." Mr. Hall paused for a minute. "Do nothing in my Nomad."

"They ain't gonna hurt theyselves if they ain't nothing loose," said Uncle Font. "Let's get in the woods."

Uncle Font directed and Mr. Hall drove, taking the Nomad down a series of logging roads, each one fainter than the one before. The last one looked as though it had not been used in a year. Pulpwooders had cut it long before, and except for occasional hunters and lost berrypickers, the last real traffic had stopped a decade ago. Pine saplings up two and three feet grew in the space between the ruts, and three or four times B.J. and the man in the red plaid shirt had to dismount and pull fallen timber out of the roadway before the pickup could go on. Each time they did, the pack of cat hounds in the living compartment broke into a storm of baying, the deep bass of Johnny Cash setting the tune and the high clamor of Johnny Ray picking out the melody.

Whenever it happened, Uncle Font would spin around where he was sitting crammed up against Mr. Hall and hammer on the rear of the truck cab, cussing the dogs by name and spraying Cotton Boll fumes over the side of Mr. Hall's head. Mr. Hall had broken a good sweat under his camouflage suit and was beginning to feel increasingly nervous about the cat-hunting pack swarming in among all the portable beds, canned goods and kitchen utensils in the Nomad living compartment.

"They certainly are lively," he remarked at one point to Uncle Font just after the old hunter had called Goddam Son-of-a-Bitch every kind of a goddamn son-of-a-bitch for causing a major collapse of several objects just behind the heads of the people riding in the pickup cab.

"Yeah," said the old man, "they having a time. I believe they purely love being in that little house back yonder. Just listen at them tussling with one another."

About then, the dim logging road petered out completely in a burned-out clearing covered with blackened pine stumps, waist-high huckleberry bushes and saw-briers. Mr. Hall killed the engine, and everybody unloaded and began looking around in the rapidly fading light. The tops of the long-needle pines were already disappearing into the night sky, and by the time Uncle Font had let the dogs out of the back of the pickup there was barely enough light left to make out details in the burned-over clearing.

"So this is the forest primeval," said Mr. Hall's friend and lifted a pint of whiskey to his lips.

"What did he say?" asked B.J.

"Norman reads a whole lot," said Mr. Hall, switching on the light in the rear of the Nomad and cautiously sticking his head inside to estimate the damage. It wasn't as bad as he thought it would be and he came out in a minute, smiling, and reached for the whiskey bottle.

"He says things like that all the time. Gets them out of books."

"Uh huh," said B.J. and checked the action of his .22 rifle. Satisfied, he set it against a stump and began watching Uncle Font tying a rope around Johnny Ray's neck. He had finished with the curse-word dog and Johnny Cash, and Elvis waited on his haunches near the old man, patiently bobbing and weaving in time to the music only he could hear.

"Some people question a Baptist preacher hunting," B.J. announced to the clearing, "but the reason I like to come on cat hunts with Uncle Font every year about this time is to get out into nature and look around for signs of God."

Nobody said anything. The book-reader took a measured sip of whiskey.

"You can sense His presence out in the woods like this," B.J. went on. "He talks to us in the movement of the breeze and the motions of the animals."

"You fellers," said Uncle Font, getting the last rope tied and beginning to fiddle with the carbide light attached to his hat by an elastic strap, "get your pants stuck down inside your boots. They're crawling tonight, and I don't want to have to call off my dogs to take one of y'all to the hospital for snakebite."

He let the four dogs pull him toward the thicket at the edge of the clearing and called back over his shoulder. "I'm fixing to cast these here dogs now, and when y'all hear Elvis sing out, come a running with your lights on."

"How'll we know it's Elvis and not one of the other ones?" asked Mr. Hall in an anxious voice and zipped something.

"Don't come for the other ones. They just background for Elvis. He got a pure sweet voice. Starts up high and then comes way down low."

The pack of hounds reached the thicket, whining, and the darkness closed around Uncle Font two steps behind them. The beam of his carbide light bobbed for a few seconds through the dense brush and was gone.

"What kind of snakes?"

"Well, up on the ridges it's rattlers," B.J. said to Mr. Hall. "Timber rattlers mainly, but I have seen a diamond-back now and then. And if the bobcat takes the dogs down into the river bottoms, why you can run into water moccasins along in there."

"I sure hope not," said Mr. Hall and turned toward the glow of his friend's cigarette end. "Where is that Old Granddad?"

B.J. walked away from the Nomad toward the far edge of the clearing. "I'm just going to step over here and listen to the woods. See if I can hear the master at work."

When he came back from taking a leak and perusing the night sky for signs of order and regularity, the two men from the Gulf coast were squatting in front of the headlights of the pickup making sure their boots were firmly fastened. Those poor fellows are depending on the courage that comes from a bottle, B.J. said to himself, and are afraid of the natural creatures God put in these woods. And one of them a declared Baptist. He ought to be ashamed of himself.

"I tell you what scares me," he said loudly, and the book-reader jumped. "It's not the serpent that crawls on his belly in God's forest." B.J. paused, and both men straightened up in his direction, blinking in the beams from the headlights. Mr. Hall had tied the ear flaps of his cap under his chin tight enough to cut into the soft flesh of his throat, and when he turned to look at B.J., the material of the cap strained under the pressure.

"No," said B.J., "it's not the rattler who warns you with the sound of his tail before he strikes or the moccasin who hisses before he bites. What I fear is the serpent who stands on two feet and comes in the night with no announcement to take your goods and the lives of you and your family."

"Oh," said Mr. Hall's friend. "You're talking about sin."

"Not exactly," answered B.J. "I'm talking about communists and hippies and doped-up colored people." He clicked the safety on and off the .22 rifle and reached in his pants pocket for the box of hollow point cartridges. "What you might call the physical presence of sin. That's what I mean."

"You get many of them up here in these woods?" asked Mr. Hall and coughed because of the tightness of the strap fastening his hat to his throat.

"Well, not yet," B.J. admitted. "But, you see, I live in Corpus Christi. I'm just up here up to preach at the Big Caney graveyard working on Sunday. Where I'm talking about the communists and dope fiends being is down in the cities. That's where they do all their crimes."

Mr. Hall switched off the pickup's headlights and the clearing plunged into darkness again, so total this time that it was a half a minute until B.J. could make out the difference between the tree line and the night sky. He could hear Mr. Hall's book-reading friend pull the cork from the bottle of Old Granddad in the silence and then make a swallowing sound.

"Was that a dog bark?" the man asked.

"No," said B.J. "You'll know when they start up." He paused for a minute. "But speaking of dogs, you fellows ever hear of Christian Guard Dogs, Incorporated?"

"What did he say?" the book-reader asked Mr. Hall. "Christian dogs?"

Before Mr. Hall could say anything, from the direction in which Uncle Font had plunged into the thicket came a drawn-out high-pitched howl, softened by distance but definitely touched by a good measure of hysteria. It hung in the air above for a few seconds and then was joined by another sound, lower in tone and divided into a series of chopping notes.

"Goddamn," said one of the Gulf coast citizens. "Excuse me preacher. What's that?"

"That first one's Johnny Ray," said B.J., "and the other one is the curse-word dog. They've hit a cat track."

The racket started up again, and within a few seconds was joined by another voice, this one beginning with a high note, descending the scale a space, hesitating, going back up for the first note, reaching it and then a bit beyond, and suddenly sliding rapidly all the way down to an ultimate bass where it held for three seconds, chopped abruptly off into silence, and then began the whole sequence all over.

"That's Elvis, and he's hot," B.J. said, fumbling with the elastic strap on his carbide light. "That's how he talks when he's close on to one. Uncle Font says he sings just the same way Elvis Presley does in that old *Don't Be Cruel* song."

B.J. got the carbide light fastened around his head on the outside of his cap, hit the switch, and the chemicals began to fizz and pop, sending a weak beam of light through the reflector which grew stronger and reached its most intense at about the time he plunged from the clearing into the thicket, his rifle held chest high.

"Hold onto what you got, and let's go," he yelled back at the two lights bobbing behind him. "We want to get there before they tree him."

Heading as best they could toward the sound of Uncle Font's pack of hounds, the three men moved through the pine thicket, stumbling over fallen logs and underbrush, catching their rifles and pieces of clothing on saw vines and creepers, stepping into rotted-out stump holes with brackish water in the bottoms, and trusting to the pale white light of the carbide.

At one point B.J. came to a brief open space and called back over his shoulder to Mr. Hall and Norman, twenty or thirty yards behind, making thrashing sounds as they tore through a clump of saw-briars and scrambled in turn over the trunk of a fallen sweet gum nearly four feet in diameter.

"Lord," he said, "don't you love this? I can just sense the eternal presence of God in this thicket."

But the cat hunters from Beaumont seemed to be too busy to answer, so B.J. spoke a couple of words in his heart to the Master and turned back toward the sounds of Elvis and Johnny Cash, louder and more impatient now as they got closer to what they were after.

In another ten minutes, B.J. reached the crest of a small hill covered with a stand of virgin pine and looked back at the two lights bobbing behind him, working their way slowly up the rise against a tide of huckleberry and yaupon bushes. Mr. Hall was saying something to Norman in a ragged voice, but was having a hard time making himself understood because of his need to pause for a deep quavery breath after every word he uttered.

"Come on," said B.J. to the carbide beams, "they're just across this next little creek. I can see Uncle Font's light, and I can hear the dogs real good."

The sound from the cat pack was now a storm of howls, bays and yips, compounded by the noises of the dogs crashing through the underbrush lining the bed of the creek as they worked the scent of the bobcat not a hundred yards ahead. Now and then came a faint yip from Uncle Font himself as he urged the dogs on by name, calling out encouragement to Goddam Son-of-a-Bitch and Johnny Ray mainly, trusting Elvis to take care of business by himself at the head of the pack.

B.J. launched himself down the hill full-tilt, crashing through brambles and sliding on pine straw, the light from his carbide light jerking from earth to sky to water as he struggled to catch up to the action. By the time he splashed through the knee-high creek and reached the other bank, the voices of the cat pack reached a new tone, one deeply touched with urgency and hysteria, and the progress of the dogs slowed, sped up for a few yards and then stopped altogether.

"He's treed," B.J. yelled back toward the men following him, just now reaching the creek and beginning to slow down for the crossing. "Look up yonder at the light on the sweet gum."

When B.J. arrived at Uncle Font's side and tilted his head back to allow the carbide beam of his lamp to shine up into the limbs of the tree which the bobcat had been forced to climb, the pack of dogs at its base was scratching around the trunk like a school of gar fish. Of the two men behind, Norman came up first, just in time to see Goddam Son-of-a-Bitch run up the bole of a fallen sycamore leaning toward the trunk of the sweet gum with no hesitation as though he expected to be able to sink his claws into the bark and scramble up the tree after the bobcat.

At this maneuver, Johnny Cash and Johnny Ray went beyond madness to a new state, baying with every breath, and beginning alternately to dig at the ground at the foot of the sweet gum and to claw at its bark as high up as they could reach. Elvis moved away three or four steps and sat back upon his haunches, peering up into the clusters of leaves and branches where the carbide lights jerked in little starts and twitches as the four hunters looked for the red eyes of the bobcat. Every few seconds the head dog barked in a low regular tune to keep the cat notified he was indeed treed, his dancing front legs moving in a quick measure, fairly close in rhythm to the beat of Presley's *That's All Right, Mama.*

"Yonder he is," said Uncle Font as a beam of light picked up two blood-red fiery points about halfway up the sweet gum just above where a large limb intersected with the trunk. "He's grinning at us."

"Where?" said Mr. Hall, "Where?" the light from his carbide lamp wobbling from one side of the mass of leaves and branches to the other as his head shook with his heavy breathing.

"Yonder," said Uncle Font and held his light steady on the face of the bobcat. "See them tushes? That thing'd eat a feller up."

"What do we do now?" asked Norman, staring up at the animal and stroking the basketball shaped belly under the front of his plaid shirt gently with one hand.

"I'm half a mind to climb up in there and punch him out in among these here dogs."

Elvis groaned deep in his throat at Uncle Font's words and increased the time of his jitterbug step close to that of *Jailhouse Rock.*

"But he's a big un," the old man continued, "and I'm scared he might cut one of them boosters up pretty bad." Uncle Font directed his light down at the pouch on the front of his bib overalls and drew out a cut of Cotton Boll tobacco. He bit off a good-sized chunk and threw his light back up into the bobcat's eyes. "Yeah, I reckon one of y'all's gonna have to shoot him on out of there."

"Which one of us gets to shoot him?" asked Mr. Hall in an

eager voice, spinning around to look at Uncle Font so that the carbide beam of his lamp shone on the old man's face.

"Y'all got to settle that for yourselves," said Uncle Font and held up a hand to keep the light out of his eyes. "It ain't nothing to me. Just aim for one of them eyes."

The bobcat in the fork of the sweet gum had just made a spitting sound at the three dogs clamoring at the base of the trunk, and B.J. had cleared his throat to enter the negotiations about who was to get to shoot when the first voice came from across the creek:

"You palefaces leave that bobcat where he is."

"Yeah," said somebody a little further down the creekbed from the first, "don't any of you fuckers shoot up in that tree."

"Lord," said B.J. and dropped his rifle into the darkness at his feet as though it had become suddenly red-hot, "who is that? Niggers?"

"I don't know," said Uncle Font, aiming the beam of his lamp toward the trees and brush across the stream and beginning to lift his .22 to his shoulder. "But I'm gonna see." The light picked up nothing but a mass of leaves and sawvines and hardwood trunks, and the first voice spoke again. "Old man," it said in deep tones which sounded definitely foreign to B.J., "you better lay that rifle down if you don't want your dogs shot full of arrows."

Clear on the opposite side of the sweet gum where the bobcat was treed somebody laughed in a high cackle which cut off abruptly in the middle.

"Oh, Jesus," said Mr. Hall and moved up a step closer to Uncle Font, "I knew it was a mistake to come out here in these woods. Yvonne tried to get me to stay home."

"What?" said Norman. "What?"

Uncle Font moved up between Johnny Cash and Johnny Ray and leaned his rifle against the hole of the sweet gum. He stepped back to where he had been, and the dogs stopped barking for a minute, sniffing at the discarded .22 and whining as though puzzled. First one, then all of the pack sat back on their haunches and looked up into the sweet gum toward the bobcat, hidden in the darkness now that the carbide beams on the men's hats had dropped to head level.

"Don't shoot no arrows into none of my dogs, niggers," said Uncle Font, directing his beam into the thicket across the creek again.

"We ain't niggers," a voice from a different location announced. "We are a war party of the Alabama-Coushatta, and this is your personal Little Big Horn, palefaces."

"Right," said the first one who had spoken. "You have done fucked with our totem, our brother the bobcat. Now you're going to have your famous last stand."

The high cackling laugh broke out again from behind the sweet gum and kept on for a full half minute this time.

"I wasn't going to shoot him," said Norman to the darkness, facing one direction and then shifting to the other. "Look, my rifle's empty. It's not even loaded." He held the weapon so that the beam of light from his carbide lamp shone on it and then jerked his hands away and let it fall to the ground in front of him.

"Here," he said, "you can have these shells." He fumbled in his pocket for his box of cartridges, found it and threw it toward the creek. It made a splash and a tinkle. "We was going to let the preacher shoot the bobcat, me and my buddy was. I mean that sincerely."

"Wait just a minute," B.J. spoke up. "I'm not here to kill anything. I just come out into the woods to study nature and praise God."

"A preacher," said one of the war party. "That means they got to have some whiskey with them."

"Hey," called another voice from a new point of the compass. "We want your firewater, palefaces."

"Here it is," Mr. Hall volunteered, pulling out what was left of the pint of Old Granddad and taking the new unopened one from Norman. "Here's all the whiskey we got."

"Put it over there on that sycamore trunk" somebody said, and Mr. Hall moved to obey, his carbide light jiggling as though he had fever. "Don't throw it in the creek like the other dumb fuck did to the shells."

"A bunch of damn reservation Indians," Uncle Font said. Elvis whined deep in his throat and barked once at the sweet gum. Two of the other dogs had flopped down to pant in the dead leaves and pine needles, and the other one, Johnny Ray, was lapping water out of the creek.

"Naw, old man," said the first voice that had spoken, "we just come in off a buffalo hunt, and our medicine's been bad."

"Shit," said Uncle Font and spit a stream of tobacco juice.

"Hush, Uncle Font," said B.J. "Don't get them mad at us."

"That's right. Listen to the preacher."

"Blessed are the peacemakers," said the Indian who had been doing all the laughing and then he laughed again.

Encouraged, B.J. spoke up. "Now what that young man just said shows you all have gone to Sunday school. Now, is this right? I ask you."

"Shut up, preacher," said somebody across the creek, making snapping noises as he moved through the brush. "We been to Sunday school and we also have seen that picture show, what's it called, He Who Watches Films?"

"*Deliverance,*" said He Who Watches Films and sniggered.

"That's right. It's all about what you rednecks do to one another when you get off in the woods together."

"Palefaces are a nasty bunch," somebody else said.

"Disgusting," came an answer in what sounded to B.J. like a put-on English accent.

"Brave, though."

"You got it," said the first voice. "Tell you soldiers what.

We as the Alabama-Coushatta war party want all y'all to take off all your clothes. All them camouflage jackets and boots and them suspenders and Fruit-of-the-Loom jockey shorts and all the rest of it."

"Oh, no," said Norman and began to sob, having seen the movie and read the book too. "What? What?"

"Don't worry, corporal," said the voice across the creek. "We ain't going to cornhole you. We ain't rednecks."

The laugher cackled again and called out: "But our necks *are* red."

"That sound like the name of a song. Our necks are red, but we ain't rednecks."

The war party began to guffaw and shake bushes, and up in the sweet gum the bobcat moved down to the next lower limb. Elvis stirred in the dead leaves and whined.

"But back to business," called the voice from across the creek. "After you palefaces get naked, call your dogs off our brother bobcat and haul ass out of here."

Mr. Hall and Norman were already pulling at their clothes, unzipping and unbuttoning as fast as they could in the wavery light from the carbide lamps, scattering garments as each piece came free. In a second B.J. joined them, bending over to untie his boots and almost tripping over the rifle he had dropped when he heard the first voice coming out of the thicket.

"You too, old man," the leader said. "What are you? Some kind of a guide to these fuckers? Get your overalls off, and all of you put your stuff in a big pile. And preacher..." the voice paused. "You the biggest man of the bunch, looking at your light. The war party wants you to carry everybody's stuff out of these woods. I mean all of it. We don't want you to leave a single damn paleface thing in these woods."

"Except for the firewater," said somebody, and the rest of them laughed.

"What about their little headlights, chief?" said the voice

behind the sweet gum.

"Y'all can wear them on out of here. You look like a bunch of one-eyed men from Mars with them things on anyway."

By this time Uncle Font's pack of hounds had noticed the bobcat's progress back down the tree and had surged forward to bay at the base of the sweet gum again, only Elvis lagging back a little.

"Shut up them dogs, old man," said the main speaker. "We got arrows trained on them just aching for their blood."

Uncle Font kicked the last leg of his overalls loose from a foot and began trying lengths of cotton rope around the neck of each dog. "Come on, dogs," he said to the cat pack. "Let him go. Let's get the goddamn hell out of this thicket."

"You tell them, Davy Crockett," said one of the war party and let out a series of high pitched yips.

Stripped to his carbide light and boots, B.J. leaned over to scoop up his and the other's clothes and rifles, and found it difficult to get everything balanced on one arm while he loaded with the other. A jacket fell off one side as he was feeling around in the dry leaves for a shirt, and somebody's rifle slipped loose when he began to straighten up.

"One of you men help me," he said in the direction of a carbide beam, and the person behind it backed off.

"They said for just you to do it," Mr. Hall warned in a shaking voice. "Uh uh. They might put an arrow through me."

"Goddamn it," said B.J., "come on and help me get out of these fucking woods."

"All right, preacher," said Mr. Hall in a shocked voice and began draping clothes over B.J.'s outstretched arm. Norman had already started off, close in the wake of Uncle Font and the four dogs, his light veering neither to the right nor left.

B.J. and Mr. Hall caught up within fifty yards, branches and vines slashing at their bare chest and legs like switches as they ran, but they didn't feel a thing. When they reached the top of the ridge paralleling the creek, they could hear sounds of splashing and yelling behind them as the war party waded across after the whiskey. They didn't look back.

Lord, prayed B.J. as he stumbled after the men and dogs in front of him, his arms dead from the weight of the clothes and guns he was carrying, you got to forgive me for taking your name in vain, but there was a whole host of devils all around me. Just get me home. Out loud he called to the naked cat hunters fleeing ahead of him:

"You got to let me tell you about Christian Guard Dogs, Incorporated. It's just this kind of thing they're a real use for." Nobody slowed, and nobody answered him all the way through the moonless thickets back to the burned-over clearing and the Nomad camper parked in the middle of it. The only sound was that of Elvis in the low bushes, moving in a steady jive.

IV

Monuments

"**Y**ou've got to dress either way down or way up for it," said the dark-haired nurse to the blonde one. "Nothing in between. That's the kind of place it is."

She pointed with her right hand to the wheelchair again without looking, and when MayBelle still didn't sit down in it, she turned away from the woman she had been addressing to see what the delay was. Her eyes were very dark and set close together. MayBelle could see that her eyebrows grew into each other in the middle but that the nurse kept a space clear between them by plucking.

"Why aren't you getting into the chair, honey?" she asked and made smoothing motions on one of the seat cushions.

"Your folks are waiting for you now."

"I don't need to be wheeled out of here," said MayBelle. "I can just walk out to that front door. I don't believe I need that chair."

"It's one real big room," the dark nurse was saying, "But it's fixed up into a bunch of little, you know, like enclosures all around the dance floor. That makes it intimate and sorta, you know, private."

"Is it high? I bet it costs an arm and a leg."

"Not if you go with the right dude," the dark nurse said and made a little wrinkle in the cleared-off space between her eyebrows.

"She's just standing there," said the blonde nurse. "Not getting in it."

The other one turned back toward MayBelle, looking just the least bit annoyed, and waved her hand in a directing motion. "Now you just get on in that chair, Miss Holt, and we'll go out there to the lobby. You've got to ride in it now. It's an official rule, and we can't break them."

Giving up, MayBelle eased herself back into the wheelchair and crossed her arms over a bundle of some sort they had given her to carry home. It was wrapped in gray paper tied with red string just the same shade as the red bumps all up and down the inside of her forearms. Looking at the raised welts made her want to scratch so she lifted her eyes to the door facing and felt the chair begin to move with her as the blonde nurse started to push from behind.

"Wait," said the old one-legged woman from the bed by the window raising herself up with one hand and pointing with the other at an empty chair against one wall. "Don't forget her little girl."

It was the only thing the woman had said since MayBelle had woken up at six in the morning and first seen her, although she had been awake the whole time cutting her eyes every few minutes over at where MayBelle lay in the steel-sided bed. MayBelle strained to look back at her from the wheelchair, but the nurse put a hand on her shoulder.

"Don't worry about old Mrs. Hudnall," she said. "She keeps seeing little girls, I guess. She says that to everybody who leaves that room."

"The light show is fantastic," said the nurse with the plucked brows. "Those strobes make it just like watching lightning strike every two seconds. People look like statues dancing."

Bubba and Avalene were waiting in the lobby along with a family of Mexicans. Bubba was wearing an orange cap with Shackleford Septic written just above the bill, and Avalene was sitting in a large gray steel and plastic chair, hands clutched to each of its arms as though she were holding herself down in the seat with great effort. She began to cry when she saw MayBelle being wheeled in by the nurses.

"Oh, Aunt MayBelle," she said in a sob, "they have just eaten you up alive." She released herself from the chair, sprang to her feet and faced the nurses. "Can't she walk?" she asked. "Has it destroyed all her nerves?"

"Oh, I'm all right, Little Sis," said MayBelle in a low voice, getting out of the wheelchair and handing Bubba the paper bundle. "Let's get on home."

"Take aholt of my arm," said Bubba, almost stepping on one of the Mexican children playing on the tile floor. "We got the truck parked real close to the building."

As they went out the door the blonde nurse was holding open, one of the bigger boys plopped himself adroitly into the wheelchair and another one leapt to push him down the hall. All the way out to the septic tank truck, MayBelle could hear the mother chattering in Mexican and delivering a series of loud slaps to the boys.

By the time Bubba had driven past the Cathedral of the

Unentombed Christ, Avalene had stopped crying and was beginning to try to get to the bottom of things. She was turned sideways in the seat by the window of the pickup so that she could see MayBelle's neck and the side of her face. MayBelle kept her gaze fixed on the tuning dial of the truck radio, and Bubba tended to his driving as he crawled along behind an overloaded pulpwood truck.

"Aunt MayBelle," said Avalene, "how did you happen to get into that bed of fire ants?"

"I didn't go to do it," MayBelle said. Bubba shifted into a lower gear.

"Well, I know that. Did you just fall down into it in the dark and couldn't get up or something?"

"It wasn't no moon last two nights," said Bubba. "Not none I could see."

"It was dark all right," agreed MayBelle and scratched at a cluster of bumps on the underside of her left wrist. That seemed to cause an itch behind her left knee so she crossed one leg over the other and rubbed them together.

"I wish y'all would look at that," Bubba said and gestured out the window at an earthmoving machine parked beside Sunflower Road. "The city is digging them sewage lines all up and down this street. They are coming inch by inch toward Mama's houses just as sure as God." He sighed gustily and eased off the accelerator so quickly the engine backfired twice, one small report and then another much louder.

"I swear I thought you was in such good shape compared to Mama, and now I just don't know," Avalene said to MayBelle's profile.

"Oh, I am," said MayBelle and stopped scratching the insect welts. "This ant business doesn't mean a thing. I just got a swimming in my head and had to sit down for a minute. It was real dark, and I couldn't see it was in a bed of fire ants."

"But why was you out yonder in the first place? In the

middle of the night and all?"

"Them wooden sticks with them plastic strings on them," said Bubba, "marks where they going to dig some more."

"It was hot in the house, and I thought I'd just see if I could get a breath of air up in the back pasture." MayBelle eased her weight more over to one side and slipped one foot in and out of its shoe. "Dust was getting all in my window from that traffic on the road. Teenagers, I guess, running their cars up and down all night long and spinning their tires in the dirt."

"You know one thing about this drought," said Bubba in a cheerful tone, "it makes the ground real hard to dig. Yesterday I had two niggers digging for a septic tank out at Soda and they went down over ten foot and ain't run into a speck of water yet. Them boys claim it's just like going through a brick sidewalk."

"Aunt MayBelle," Avalene said in a low dramatic voice and paused for effect. "That Cuban doctor said you had been drinking. Said your blood showed it."

MayBelle looked hard at a crack in the volume knob on the radio and then reached out with one hand to touch it.

"He did?"

"He sure did," said Avalene and leaned forward to look around MayBelle toward Bubba. "Can't you get us around that old pulpwood truck? We are just eating his dust."

"No, I can't," said Bubba. "I'm taking my time so I can look at progress." He hawked deep in his throat and spit out his window into the red cloud hanging in the air.

"I had taken some of my kidney medicine," said MayBelle. "Probably he just smelled that on my breath." She reached up and pushed at a barrette that had been working its way out of her hair. "Cuban," she said to the radio knob.

"But he said the blood," Avalene answered. "Not just your breath."

"That kidney medicine gets all in your blood," said Bubba. "How do you think it does you any good, Little Sis? You see, your body system, the blood part of it, is just like a septic tank set-up. It's got all these channels and holding chambers and one-way valves and gas release vents. Got these here processing parts to it and inner workings matched right up with a septic system. You understand what I'm saying?"

Bubba looked earnestly around MayBelle at Avalene and let the truck slow even further, enough so that the pulpwood vehicle ahead began to pull away.

"What I'm talking about is the exact same reason that a septic tank is superior to a central sewer set-up with all them running pipes and everything. The septic tank and the body system is just alike. They are both natural." Bubba gave the pickup a little more acceleration and faced back to the front. "And just got to be better. No, Aunt MayBelle wasn't drunk nor drinking. And a septic tank whips a sewer everytime."

"Well, that's what B.J. claims, too," said Avalene. "He won't trust a foreign doctor."

"Listen to your big brother, Avalene," MayBelle said, rubbing her back against the truck seat to get at an ant bite she couldn't reach any other way. "He knows I wasn't drinking nothing."

Nobody said anything as the pickup crested a little hill covered with rusting car bodies and jimson weed and began its descent down the other side. MayBelle squirmed slowly in the seat between her niece and nephew, fighting the desire to reach into the front of her dress and claw at her left armpit. An itch had started there which made her forget all the other ones, and she focused hard on a piece of vine hanging down from one of the pulpwood pieces on the truck ahead of Bubba's pickup to try to ignore it.

"Where is B.J.?" she asked, hoping to get a response she could think about.

"Still in bed, I reckon," said Avalene. "Watch out for that nigger car, Bubba. He came in early from hunting last night,

Mama said, and didn't speak a word to nobody. Just went straight to bed."

"Maybe he's thinking about his sermon for tomorrow," MayBelle said.

"That or them dogs," said Bubba, looking hard at a yellow Buick convertible carrying a family of blacks with his hand poised over the pickup horn. "That feller from Lufkin's going to preach at the graveyard working, too. Supposed to be a real cutter. Name's Purkett."

"I bet he ain't been to college," said Avalene.

"Probably not," admitted Bubba, "but I hear he can forever more preach up a storm."

"B.J. can take him," said Avalene. "I have no doubts about that."

"What time are we leaving in the morning for Big Caney?" asked MayBelle, trying not to think about itches.

"You ain't going, Aunt MayBelle," said Avalene. "You been in the hospital. You're sick."

"Oh, yes, I am, too, Little Sis," said MayBelle in a clear voice, sitting up straight and uncrossing her legs with so much energy that she kicked Bubba's accelerator foot hard enough to hurt.

"Well, we'll have to see," said Avalene and began to hum the opening bars of *The Old Rugged Cross*. She had gotten almost to the chorus by the time Bubba swung the nose of the septic tank truck into the gravel driveway of Myrtle's yard and parked behind B.J.'s Oldsmobile. He killed the engine and MayBelle reached for her hospital bundle, but Avalene put her hand on her arm to stop her.

"Wait a minute, Aunt MayBelle," she said. "We want to talk to you a little bit about Mama." She looked over at Bubba sitting behind the wheel under his orange septic tank service cap. "Idn't that right?"

"Yeah, Aunt MayBelle," said Bubba. "You know, the kind

of shape she's in and everything. The condition her mind's in and all like that."

"Kids," said MayBelle, taking a deep breath and looking from one to the other, "her mind's just like it's always been. Only more so now."

Everybody sat still for a minute to let two City of Annette dump trucks roar past, running in close tandem up Sunflower Road, and then Bubba and Avalene began speaking at the same time in low fast tones.

"See," said Bubba, "the thing is, Aunt MayBelle, about Mama..."

"What we think we got to do, you understand," Avalene was saying as both raised their voices to be heard over the other, louder and louder until both quit at the same time.

"Bubba," said Avalene in the sudden silence, "will you let me talk for just one minute? You have never listened to anybody in your life."

"All right, OK. Talk on. I'll just set here 'til you're finished and then I'll tell it the right way."

"Let me talk then." Avalene turned her attention to MayBelle again and rolled up the window on her side of the pickup. "I bet Mama's moved up to that screen door to see what we're doing out here."

"Naw," said MayBelle. "She's watching one of her shows on the Dumont this time of the morning. Go on ahead."

"Me and Bubba have been talking for a long time about how she's doing and how bad off she's got," said Avalene, turning her head back and forth to look at the front of the house and then at MayBelle. "And we have decided it's time to do something about it."

"Yeah," Bubba said. "High time."

"Hush, Bubba. We are going to talk some more with B.J. this afternoon and try to arrange things for next week."

MayBelle shifted her bundle to the other hand and didn't say anything. The temperature in the truck was steadily rising with Avalene's window rolled up, and she felt sweat beginning to trickle from each armpit over the tender places where the ants had stung her. Her left side just above her waistline began to burn.

"Here's what we want to ask you to do. Now you've been living with Mama for a long time, and you can tell when she's changed and how she used to be."

"I've been here fifty-one years, and I've seen lots of changes and lots of things staying the same."

"That's what I mean," said Avalene. "You're able to judge better than anybody else. And that's what they're going to want you to do."

"Who is?"

"The people at the courthouse," Avalene said and jerked her head around to look at the door to Myrtle's house.

"And at the state place too," Bubba added.

"Where?" MayBelle asked.

"State hospital. That's what we talking about here," said Bubba.

"That's where Mama's going to have to go."

"Oh," MayBelle said and looked through the truck windshield at the crepe myrtle beside the driveway. Sitting in its highest limb was a mockingbird, opening its wings, stretching them to the limit until their white undersides were completely revealed, and then folding them again to its sides in a regular pattern as though the whole thing were a dance set to music.

"Look at that mockingbird," said MayBelle, "fanning himself. He looks too hot and tired to try to fly."

"Forget that bird yonder," said Bubba. "Will you help us get Mama put away?" He paused for a minute. "Or not?"

MayBelle watched the white underside of the mockingbird's wing come into view, vanish and reappear twice more, and then she turned toward Avalene. Her niece had a thick line of sweat

105

across her upper lip.

"All right," she said, her eyes fixed on the beads of water. "I'll do it then. Take my bundle, Bubba."

"I swear I saw them again last night. They had little lights fixed on their heads, but when they turned right toward you, you couldn't see them no more."

Myrtle took a long drink from the glass of iced tea in her right hand and rebalanced it with a thump on the arm of her rocker.

"I was too scared to breathe almost. Wasn't nobody here with me. You was off in the hospital and B.J. off hunting in the woods, and Lord knows where Avalene was. All I could do was sit here in the dark and pray."

"Did you call the sheriff's office again?"

"No. Would they believe me? Do they ever believe me?" Myrtle stared over the rim of her glasses at MayBelle with a hurt look and answered her own question. "No, they never do. Besides, I was afraid they would hear the clicking outside when I dialed the telephone and come on in here and point their little instruments at me or something." She lifted her eyes to the sideways picture of Burton in his coffin above the Dumont and gestured toward it with her iced tea.

"No," she said, "I didn't call nobody. I just did something I hope I don't go to Hell for. Please Jesus."

"What was that?" asked MayBelle, roused from picking at a cluster of ant bites behind her left knee by the statement. "What was it you say you did?"

Myrtle had first started seeing the lights almost a year ago, right around Labor Day weekend. Sitting up in bed one night after the Dumont screen started showing nothing but snow and static, she had leaned propped against two pillows, listening to the green and yellow fluids seethe and bubble just below her breastbone and praying for the blessed relief that almost always came just when it seemed things in her chest were about to reach a boil. She turned out the bedside lamp, and after her eyes adjusted to the dark she saw the first one, a weak flash that brightened and faded and moved in figure eights outside the front window of the bedroom, coming nearer to the house and backing off until finally it vanished as though a switch had been turned off.

After that first sighting, the lights began coming in twos and threes, once as high as seven, moving randomly at first in little clusters and jerks until finally right around Christmas they began to arrange themselves in what looked to Myrtle like patterns. "First one, then another one will kind of dance off to one side and jiggle up and down for a minute," she said to the lady who answered the telephone at the sheriff's office at night. "Then the other ones will all go over yonder with that first one and then start the whole business all over again. Y'all got to come out and arrest them things."

"All right, Mrs. Shackleford," the telephone woman would say, "we'll send the patrol car out yonder to Sunflower Road."

And several times, one of the deputies would crawl into the Pontiac cruiser and roar out to Myrtle's house, lights flashing and tires spinning in the gravel roadbed.

"Hot flashes," Sheriff Jimmy Youngblood would tell the deputy when he reported over his CB radio that he couldn't find a thing out of the way on Sunflower Road. "Either that, or mean boys having a good time with some hand spotlights. Just tell her you looked around, and come on back to the courthouse."

Finally even the deputy got tired of roaring out to the Shackleford place in the Pontiac and began parking in an alley behind Cockran's Department Store and calling in his reports from there. "Ain't nothing," he would say to Estelle on the other end of the radio. "Just a dark night and them damn female flare-ups."

Once after she had called the sheriff's number and crouched down behind a chifferobe waiting for an hour for the deputy to flush the moving lights out of her side yard and no one had ever come, Myrtle crawled back to the telephone across the cold hardwood floor and dialed again.

"I used to be proud to tell anybody I was from Annette, Texas," she said in a low venomous whisper to the telephone lady in the sheriff's office. "Now I'm ashamed to admit to a soul where I come from. When they ask me where I live, I just don't say nothing. I got a good mind to tell folks I live in Corrigan or Diboll or even Woodville."

From that point on, she took to sleeping under a feather mattress each night, pulling the thick comforter up over her as she sat up in bed, no matter how hot it was in the house. She would wake in the morning drenched with sweat, not sure whether she had actually seen or just dreamed the cluster of lights that had dipped and moved in intricate patterns outside her windows during the dead hours of midnight.

"If Youngblood can't find nothing out yonder, Mama," B.J. told her, "maybe it ain't nothing but niggers roaming through the night."

"It ain't niggers, I don't think," she had said. "It's lights. They wouldn't have lights. But either way, I'm losing weight from all this sweating under that feather comforter. Just look at the size of your moother's poor arms. Feel underneath my neck how hot I am. Just like I'm burning up with the fever."

Myrtle took a long sip at her glass of iced tea and pointed up at Burton's picture again. "Him," she said. "Right up there."

"What about him?" said MayBelle. "He's still causing trouble, is he?"

"No, he's not causing trouble. I believe he might have saved my life last night, wherever he is in heaven."

"Wherever Burton Shackleford is," MayBelle said, "He is causing all the commotion he can think to do. You can bank on that."

"You would say something like that. And with all he did for you."

"I wish he hadn't done so much for me. I'd be a lot better off now if he hadn't done half of what he did."

"I prayed to him last night when them lights commenced to bobbing and dancing in the yard and me all by myself," said Myrtle and paused for a minute to shift her weight in the oak rocker to a better spot. "And he answered my prayer," she said in a triumphant tone. "Right here in the house he built with his own hands."

"God?"

"No," snapped Myrtle. "Burton Shackleford. My dead husband. My second husband."

"That'd be the first time he ever give anybody something they asked for. Burton wasn't known for giving people things. Not when he was alive."

Myrtle reared back in her chair, pushing hard with both feet on the little stool she kept in front of the rocker, and fixed MayBelle with a look of steel. She stared for fully half a minute before she spoke.

"I'm thinking about Houston," she said with a fine deliberateness. "I'm remembering Houston, Texas."

"What about Houston? It gets real hot down there. Real muggy with all that water in the air. That's what Houston means to me."

"You know what I'm talking about. That time when you had to make your little trip down yonder. When was it now? Forty some odd years now, I believe it's been."

"It's forty-five years this coming November," MayBelle said and looked at Burton in his peaceful pose above the Dumont console. "Forty-five years on the seventh of the month."

"Yes sirree," said Myrtle, rocking her head until the light flashed from her glasses like a signal going off and on, "that was one time you owed Burton Shackleford for something, and you can't deny it."

"There's some things you better hope I keep on denying," MayBelle said in a blurred voice. "Big sister, I'd watch myself if I was you. Which, thank the Lord, I ain't."

"I don't have to worry about nothing with him watching over me," Myrtle answered and pointed a finger at the serene picture of Burton. "He's my direct line to Heaven. Him and the Holy Ghost."

"He looks awful dead to me, slumping down in that coffin."

"He ain't slumped down in that coffin," Myrtle said with heat. "It just looks that way because it's turned sideways, and you know it. He's lying there at his own natural full length."

Both sisters fell silent and looked away from the other, MayBelle at a withered blossom on the yellow rose bush visible through the window and Myrtle at the adjustment knobs of the Dumont television set. Back in the kitchen Avalene was making cooking noises, and Bubba was saying something that made her laugh. A pickup passed on Sunflower Road, and as the cloud of red dust it kicked up billowed up against the front door screen, MayBelle changed the subject.

"What do you suppose all them lights are you see at night around here, Myrtle?"

"Well," began Myrtle in a low voice calculated not to let her children hear, but one which rose in volume as she went on, "I told you already before, but I'll repeat myself. I believe to my soul it's some kind of a visit from out there." She pointed in the direction of the ceiling and looked over her shoulder toward the back part of the house. "I been watching all these special news shows on the TV and it all fits into what they tell about."

"You mean ghosts or spirits?"

"No, no. I think it's things from another world. You know, a different planet from this one. I believe it's some creatures from one of these flying saucers that people been seeing everywhere these last few years."

"You do? What makes you think that?"

"Their little hats," Myrtle said simply. "The way they glow with them strange colored lights and how they move in them little designs all around the house."

"Designs? I don't believe you mentioned designs to me before."

"Yes, I did. I believe they are giving signals by the way they move around. Flashing back directions to the mother ship."

"How do you figure that?" asked MayBelle, rubbing her left leg against the arm of the oak rocker to get at a bunch of ant stings that she had previously scratched raw with her fingernails.

"Sometimes right before the little lights begin to show up and move around, it comes a great big glow right over the house like there was a big thing just a setting over the roof top sending out beams. I figure that's the ship they all come out of."

"Uh huh," said MayBelle.

From out in the dog pen came the sound of a high-pitched yip, followed by several barks and then a whole chorus of deep-throated growls and howling. Somebody yelled, and then another different voice joined in, saying a word MayBelle couldn't quite catch over and over again.

"Who's that out yonder with the dogs?" she asked.

"B.J. and that nigger."

"Which nigger?"

"Old Sully," said Myrtle. "The very one that woke them boys up in their tent and had them come haul you out of that bed of ants."

"What's B.J. got that poor old nigger doing?"

"Step to the window and see. B.J. says he believes if he

trains them Christian guard dogs with a live nigger they'll get mean like they're supposed to and maybe get to be worth something."

MayBelle walked to the window, lifted the shade back and stood to one side so she could see out. In the far corner of the pen Sully was standing with his back to the fence, facing two of the German shepherds which were moving slowly toward him with their tails dropped and the hair down their backbones raised straight up. He was wearing a heavy gray overcoat that came to his ankles, work gloves up to his elbows and B.J.'s Johnny Bench catcher's mask over his face.

B.J. leaned over the fence from behind Sully and said something to him, and the little man raised one hand to eye level and, as B.J. spoke again, all the way above his head. At that movement, the shepherd nearest the fence launched itself at Sully without making a sound, and snagged a mouthful of overcoat in its jaws just at the man's chest level. Sully staggered forward off-balance, and the other shepherd hit, seizing one of the work gloves in its teeth, and as it stripped it off the man's hand, beginning to worry the thing in the dust of the pen as though it had a cat down, snapping its head from side to side in short sudden jerks.

"'Lectric, 'lectric," Sully yelled, feeling himself toppling forward with the weight of the dog dangling from his overcoat. "'Lectric, Reverend Shackleford. 'Lectric."

"Drag him toward the fence some," said B.J. fumbling with the switch on the cattle prod as he stuck the instrument through the strands of hogwire. "I can't reach him from here with you way over yonder."

Sully fell to both knees, dislodging the shepherd, and scrambled backwards on all fours toward the fence, begging for electricity the whole way. By the time the dog worrying the work glove had given it up and turned to join the other one working its way toward Sully, B.J. had managed to get his cattle prod into operating position and was kneeling with it extended and ready.

"Let them come on now, Sully," he said. "Make a face at them or something and get them to jump at you."

"Lord have mercy, my face don't want to do nothing but get out of this dog pen."

"Aw, you got your catcher's mask on and everything," said B.J. and hit the cattle prod switch, causing a little blue spark about a half inch long to leap out of its end. "They are *not* going to hurt you none. Now stand on up and wave your arms around again."

At sight of the cattle prod both German shepherds rapidly gave ground fast enough to kick up twin clouds of red dust, and didn't stop their retreat until they had backed all the way into the group of other dogs ranged against the fence behind them.

"They see that little 'lectric spark," said Sully and reached down to pick up the chewed work glove. "Who wee. Looky here where his old teeth done broke through this here leather."

"That's right," said B.J. "that's the only thing they respect and fear. This electric cattle prod and me."

"Uh huh," said Sully and looked longingly toward the gate cut into the side of the fence. "You reckon you could let me out for a while now, Reverend?"

"In a minute, in a minute. Yes sir, I believe these dogs are getting mean enough now to face down any kind of a communist or a hippie."

B.J. looked into the swirling pack at the far end of the pen with satisfaction. The dogs were milling about restlessly with their tails dropped, each one careful to keep out of the path of the other ones, yet too keyed up to quit moving and flop down onto the dusty ground.

"Yes sir," B.J. announced, "they are not afraid of a hippie."

"I hope there ain't no hippie come around here none with a cattle prod," said Sully.

"Huh," said B.J. and flicked his switch on and off a couple of times. "Hippies don't know a thing about cattle prods. Besides, Christian Guard Dogs is not for up here in the country where folks use prods. It's for in the cities where all the robbers and murderers live. You ought to know that, Sully."

"Yes sir, Reverend Shackleford. I imagine you know what you're talking about all right." Sully stopped talking and eased a little to his left along the fence as close to it as he could press himself and still move. "You reckon you could watch me with that 'lectric stick up to that gate yonder, sir?"

"All right," said B.J. "We'll take us a break now."

Back in the house MayBelle leaned closer to the window and spoke over her shoulder to Myrtle.

"Everytime Sully takes a step along that fence, them dogs take a step along the other side of it."

"They do?" asked Myrtle. "That's good. I expect they are learning to mistrust a nigger."

"Or a cattle prod one."

MayBelle let the shade fall back and crossed the room to her chair. "I don't know if that's right to do that kind of thing."

"What? Train them guard dogs to take care of Christian families? Why, you know it's just the kind of a project B.J. would come up with to help folks out. He's just like his daddy was that way."

"No, I mean to scare an old man like that with them mean dogs. He must be older than you are by now."

"Well, I should hope he is," said Myrtle and belched loudly. "Thank you, sweet Jesus." Relieved, she leaned back in the oak rocker and propped both feet up on the little stool in front of her.

"Niggers are naturally afraid of dogs. B.J. ain't going to let them hurt him none. They might make him skip around a little, but that won't bother him a bit."

"I don't see B.J. on but one side of that fence," MayBelle said, "and I don't have to say which one neither."

"B.J. is paying that lazy old man. He ain't doing a thing he don't want to do, and besides he's in good health and can step lively when he has to."

Myrtle sat quietly for a minute staring at the dead screen of the Dumont with a pensive look on her face as though she were listening to another episode in the eternal struggle in her lower bowels.

"MayBelle," she asked in a troubled voice, "why is it the Lord will give health to an old nigger man like Sully and make a white lady like me suffer from all these pressures and strains inside? It don't seem right hardly, me with my children and responsibilities and can't get no help and that old gray-headed coon able to fight off them guard dogs at his age. I tell you sometimes it makes me want to question my Savior's judgment."

"Maybe He figures Old Sully's got more use for good health than some people. You ever think about that?"

"No," said Myrtle. "I don't think about stuff that don't make sense, and that's what most of what you say amounts to." She raised herself in the rocker and tilted to one side so that most of her weight was on one haunch, allowing her to get some relief from the mounting pressure within.

"He," she said, pointing to the casket shot above the Dumont, "knew niggers, and he knew you. Burton Shackleford said there wasn't one worth shooting in a boxcar load."

"Burton Shackleford said a whole lot of things," said MayBelle. "And he said every one of them a whole lot of times. Yes indeed, he was always saying something."

"Smart aleck," said Myrtle.

Both sisters fell silent and listened to the sounds Avalene was making in the kitchen and to the growls and yips B.J. was causing in the dog pen outside. MayBelle's bites itched, she was thirsty and she felt as though the dust rising and blowing things through the front door screen each time a car passed on the road was aimed directly at her. She looked down at the arm of her chair and drew a little circle with the tip of her finger in the film settled on it. In less than minute she could see new specks gathering in the clear spot she had made.

"I don't know what I'm going to wear to Big Caney," she said.

"I do," Myrtle said.

Two boys on bicycles rode slowly by the house headed up Sunflower Road, and Sully said something to B.J. or to a Christian guard dog in the side yard. Slipping one hand into the front of her dress, MayBelle clawed at an ant bite hidden beneath a slip strap and held back a groan when it wouldn't stop itching.

"What?" she asked finally.

"My black dress with the open embroidery worked across the bust line."

"It's going to be hot."

"Not with them little airholes."

"They don't let that much air through."

"Enough to cool me off."

"Mama and Aunt MayBelle," said Avalene, "y'all come on and eat."

Bubba looked out of the corner of his eye at his mother and took a sip of coffee. "Oo-wee, he said. "Everybody's sick. Aunt MayBelle ant-bit and Mama's still got her stomach problems."

"All down in my legs too," said Myrtle and lifted both feet from the floor so she could stretch them toward Bubba's end of the table. "It runs from the joint of my hip all the way down to the tips of my toes, the pain does."

"You sleep all right last night, Mama?" Avalene asked in a

bright voice.

"Not hardly."

"Why's that now?" said Bubba. "The same old business?"

"I was all by myself in that front bedroom, just a burning up under that comforter and them lights just dancing all night from midnight on."

"It was the same ones, you think?" Bubba said.

"I don't know if it was the same ones or not, but they were sure from the same place."

"Now, Mama," said Avalene, "you know better than that."

"Avalene, honey, you're just a child and don't know a thing about it," said Myrtle in a pitying tone. "I pray to God it never happens that such things ever come to plague you in the night."

"Ain't nothing never plagues Avalene in the night," Bubba said. "No matter how close she looks for it, neither." He leaned over and punched his sister lightly high up on the shoulder.

"Leave her alone, Bubba," said MayBelle before Avalene could answer. "I imagine nighttime is right peaceable for everybody around this table. And I imagine it has been for a while."

"It was a pattern," said Myrtle, "just a flashing right through that feather comforter and on into my eyelids even. Like when lightning would strike, back when it used to rain in Coushatta County."

"I hate to break into this discussion," B.J. said, "just when it was getting around to something interesting. But I got to tell you all how things are going to be tomorrow at the graveyard working."

The session with the guard dogs had left B.J.'s hair plastered to his forehead as though he had poured a bucket of water over himself, and he felt still hot enough to melt the ice cubes in his tea glass by touching it with just two fingers. He fixed his eyes level and swept his gaze around the table until everybody but MayBelle was looking at him. The quicker he got the bickering between Avalene and Bubba quieted down and Myrtle's revelations about dancing lights stopped the sooner he could get things organized and some peace to cool off in.

"Avalene," he said in a sweet voice, "you and Bubba and Aunt MayBelle are going to ride in Bubba's pickup, and Mama and Barney and me are going in the Olds."

"I'm not riding that back seat," Myrtle said and slapped her fork down hard enough to knock some crowder peas off her plate onto the table. MayBelle watched two of them roll to the edge and drop to the floor.

"One, two," she said. "Buckle my shoe."

B.J. reached out and put his hand over his mother's.

"Now, Mama. When have I ever made you sit anywhere but in the front seat of my car?"

"Everytime Peachie's here and we go somewhere," she answered flatly.

"Well, you're going to be riding in the front seat with me tomorrow all the way to Big Caney, and Barney Lee will be in the back. And the rest of us," he waved his unengaged arm in a loose circle, "will be going in Bubba's truck hauling the dogs in the trailer."

"Wait a minute," said Bubba. "You mean you intend for me to pull that sheet metal trailer all the way to Big Caney behind my Shackleford Septic pickup?" He stopped talking to gaze wide-eyed at B.J.

"Why, Big Brother, you know that thing's going to make both them left tires wear uneven."

"I'm asking you to help me, Bubba," said B.J., pulling his hand away from Myrtle's to get at the serving spoon in the squash bowl. "It'll mean a lot to Christian Guard Dogs to show up out there with that trailer load of Dobermans and shepherds."

"You carrying them dogs to Big Caney?" said MayBelle. "Why? There ain't no terrorists hanging around the graveyard last I heard."

"Why, Aunt MayBelle," said Avalene, "I see you don't know business promotion."

"Business what?" said Myrtle. She has always loved to hear one of her children use a new phrase picked up at school or downtown Annette. Avalene had learned this one while she was working under Mr. Boyd Purvis last Friday in the little backroom in Goodrich, and she was now pleased to share it.

"Business promotion," she said. "What it means, Mama and y'all, is positioning yourself as a commercial enterprise to get the best return on what you got to offer."

"Did you learn that at Drews Business College, Little Sis? asked Bubba, who had never had the educational opportunities of his brother and sister, being born as he had been right between them and therefore never getting any show.

"I bet she did," said Myrtle proudly. "Little Sis will pop a new word on you as regular as shelling peas."

"No," said Avalene, "not this time. It comes from on-the-job experience."

"Y'all talk about dogs a lot down there at the lumber company in Goodrich," asked MayBelle, "do you?"

"No, we don't talk about dogs, Aunt MayBelle. These here business concepts apply to everything."

"No doubt about it," said MayBelle and leaned forward in her chair to ease a dress seam away from an ant bite.

"Yes, ma'am," said B.J. moving to recapture the conversation, "it's a wonderful opportunity for Christian Guard Dogs. Having all the dogs down there for folks to look at."

"But, son," said Myrtle, "is that right to have them dogs a barking and carrying on at a graveyard working? Won't people say it's not reverent? I know your daddy would have never let a dog inside a church house." Myrtle leaned back to get a better chance at easing some grumbling internal pressure and gestured with a quivering hand. "I can say it right here. Burton

Shackleford would have never carried no living animal of no kind into the house of God."

"Why, Mama," said Avalene, "don't you know B.J. would never do nothing to offend the Lord? This is business."

"Let me explain it, Little Sis," B.J. broke in. "This whole project, Mama, is so Christians will be protected from evil people that want to do them harm and take off their property and sell it in Houston and Beaumont. What I'm doing by demonstrating my guard dogs is a Christian act of charity."

"Yeah," said Bubba. "And we might sell one or two of them boosters if they act mean enough."

"Oh, they're going to act mean," B.J. said. "Don't you worry about that. We are going to have somebody else going out there with us to take care of that part of the program."

Everybody at the table swung around to look directly at B.J., all the eyeglasses focusing together like a cluster of insect eyes suddenly finding something of common interest to consider.

"Who?" asked Avalene.

"Sully," said MayBelle.

"Naw," said Myrtle. "Naw, son, you ain't going to take a nigger to Big Caney to the graveyard working. Not out there where your dead daddy's laying buried."

"Yes, Mama," B.J. answered. "I am. And I can explain it to you so you'll see just how right it is to do what I'm going to do."

"He will," said MayBelle. "He will explain it. I ain't seen it fail yet."

"Aunt MayBelle," said Avalene. "Just listen and hush."

"Demonstration," B.J. began, "is the first step toward persuasion. Old Sully working these Christian Guard Dogs is just in the same category as Jesus feeding the multitude with the loaves and fishes."

It's always after it's already decided that the talking comes, Maybelle thought. They always claim that the talk is first and then the thing happens, but what it really is is the thing is already done and the explaining why it has to be done begins then. So they are really lying twice to you. Lying when they say it's not done yet and lying when they explain why it has to be done.

And there's a whole lot of movement to lying to you too. Sometimes you see the hands gesturing and explaining and building a thing in the air that they want you to see, and when they're really good at lying, you don't even notice the movement, but it's always there. The hands moving and the mouth and the eyes. B.J.'s good at it, but you can always see the movements. B.J.'s not as good as he was. He always moved so you couldn't see it.

That time in Houston I couldn't even tell whether he was saying it or I was thinking it. It was like your hand sliding over a white silk blouse in one of the big stores there. It went on and on until it was in the air touching nothing before you knew it, and you wanted to go back and let it slide over it again and again because you really couldn't believe it had stopped since you didn't know it started. And with him, something was always moving, but I never could catch it, and it was gone before I even knew it was there.

The turn off the black top road was always hard to find. It always seemed like the way to Big Caney had moved since last time, and it wasn't until you had gone past the pear trees in the front yard of Old Man Tom Blanchard's place that you could see you were on the right way to it again.

In August at graveyard working time the pears were ripe enough to pull for canning, but they were too hard to eat even when I was young and had good teeth. But that April when just the blossoms were showing white against the pale green leaves, he stopped the car and pulled off a limb just full of flowers and gave it to me. That was when Mr. Blanchard was still living in the house place, but he didn't see us stopped because it was before noon and he would have been ploughing way on down in the bottom somewhere.

By the time we drove back by the pear trees that night, most of the blooms had fallen, and I was finding them withered in the floorboard and the backseat for the next week. She asked me where they had all come from when we went to a singing at the church the next Wednesday, and I said I guess some wind just blew them in the open window. She said you're lucky it didn't get wet in your car, and I said it did.

"Listen to them bark, said Bubba. "They just a carrying on, bouncing all over that trailer on this old washboard road."

"Didn't they use to grade out here some?" said Avalene, twisting in her seat to get some distance between her and the center hump of Bubba's pickup as it surged up to slap her bottom again.

"Aw, yeah. But they ain't no more votes out here in the county. Everybody's done moved to Annette and wanting city sewage hookup. Them commissioners don't care about nothing no more but water pumping through plastic pipes."

Bubba looked past Avalene's nose toward MayBelle, leaning forward over the steering wheel to seek some sign of confirmation.

"Ain't that right, Aunt MayBelle?"

"What? Are you talking to me? I can't hear nothing in all this uproar."

"Oh, that's OK." said Bubba and cleared his throat pensively. "Just set to your seat, and we'll be there directly."

"This here truck ride is kind of hard on Sully," MayBelle stated, peering around to look through the back window at the little black man balancing himself in a metal and plastic lawnchair in the bed of the pickup.

"He's used to jouncing," said Avalene. "I bet he's having

himself a high old time coming to the white folks' graveyard working."

"What I understand," MayBelle said, "he ain't used to jouncing on no truck bed."

"Don't you start talking that way, now Aunt MayBelle. We're all going to have us a nice and pleasant time out at the cemetery."

Avalene cut her eyes over at Bubba and leaned into his shoulder to get his attention.

"Isn't that right, Bubba? No talking about bad things or saying stuff that people might not like to hear."

Avalene had learned from experience in the business world that if you put ideas in somebody's head before they might do something you didn't want them to, lots of times they wouldn't.

"We're just going to sing," she went on, "and pull weeds and eat good cooking and have ourselves just the best old time."

"I'm ready for it," said Bubba. "I've just been worrying myself sick about them pipelines reaching everywhere in Annette. All up and down the roads. Even plain old dirt roads like this one." He took one hand off the wheel to point to the gravel road bed ahead, and as he did he ran the pickup over a chughole big enough to make everything and everybody in the vehicle leave their resting places and become airborne.

"Bubba," said Avalene, holding her right hand to her side just below where her bra cut into it, "Jesus Christ! Watch where you're driving."

"Look at them guard dogs and old Sully," said Bubba, eyes fixed in the rearview mirror. "They're all lying down and getting up. And then lying down and getting up."

"You better not have hurt none of them dogs," said MayBelle. "Your preaching brother will break your neck for you."

"Oh, no," said Avalene. "Just look at that dirt in the air."

The pickup was moving into a hanging cloud of red clay dust kicked up by a vehicle somewhere ahead, and both Bubba and MayBelle began cranking their window handles.

"Well, slow down, Bubba," said Avalene, blowing her breath out in quick little pants to keep the dust from settling on her upper lip. "You're not obliged to run on up there into it. Just look at my organdy dress."

MayBelle finished rolling up the window and looked down at her own clothes, the white collar against the pale green bodice of the dress. I can see on through where it's buttoned to the age spots on my chest, she thought, bad as my eyes have got with these old glasses. You can see the red dust beginning to gather at the edge of the seams on the collar the further on we go. I was never big like she was, but he said he loved the way my skin looked. It's so white, he said, so white everywhere and not a mark on it.

"I don't know what's worse," said Bubba, "eating that pulpwood truck's dust or burning up in the cab of this pickup with all these windows rolled up." He slapped at the sides of his face with his free hand, first on the right cheek, then the left.

"You ought to get this thing air-conditioned," said Avalene. "I don't know why B.J. made me ride to the graveyard working in this old septic tank truck." Her voice had suddenly gathered so much whine in it that it seemed likely that she would burst into tears with her next breath.

"Now, Little Sis, you know exactly why he's back there with Mama and you're riding with me. B.J.'s trying to talk to her about the advantages of living in an institution."

"Well, she's not about to volunteer to go get in one. I don't care what you and B.J. think about talking to her about it."

"Aw, hell, Avalene, we know that," Bubba said. "He's just offering it to her in front of a witness so later on when we get her committed Barney Lee can swear he heard us trying to reason with her."

"You might as well try to put a side saddle on a hog as try to reason with Myrtle," MayBelle said. "I believe that reason gives her the colic."

"Now, Aunt MayBelle," Avalene said in a sweet lilt, "you remember what we all said about talking nice and making everybody love us?"

"Talking ain't got nothing to do with love," said MayBelle. "But I will try to keep your kind advice in mind."

"Do that," sang Avalene.

Up ahead the cloud of red grew even thicker for a space and then as if at a signal began abruptly to thin and settle. As it did, MayBelle could see the first car pulled over to the shoulder of the dirt road, a new blue big one with a tall antenna rising up from the center of its trunk. She lifted her gaze to the skyline and narrowed her eyes to begin to pick out the tops of the cedars from among the pine and sweet gum trees lining the sides of the road.

"Big Caney," she said out loud. "Graveyard working again."

"Look at all them cars and trucks," said Bubba, slowing the pickup to a crawl. "They parked further back this year than I ever seen it."

"Get that window down," said Avalene, "and watch out for them two kids in the road. It's because of the two preachers."

"What is?" asked Bubba, bringing the pickup to a stop and beginning to look around for an open space to nose into.

"All the extra cars this year. They're here because of B.J. and that Lufkin fellow, Purkett."

As Bubba maneuvered the pickup between two parked cars, shifting back and forth from low to reverse and throwing Dobermans and shepherds from side to side of the trailer in the process, MayBelle tried to see what the two children were playing with just outside the truck. They had moved out of the road and were now down on their knees in the shallow ditch beside it looking at something one of them was holding as though it were something priceless that might get away. Both boys were wearing Dallas Cowboy T-shirts, and both had hair so blonde it was almost white in the sunlight. If it was fifty years ago, MayBelle thought, those boys would probably have their heads shaved for ringworm and they'd be wearing home-made overalls.

"Well," said Bubba and cut the engine. "Got her off the road and the backend pointed in the right direction."

MayBelle leaned closer to the windshield to see, shading the glass with her left hand to make it easier. Whatever it was was moving, and now both boys had their hands on it.

"What you see, Aunt MayBelle? Cute little boys playing in the ditch? I bet it reminds you of your nieces and nephews."

"In a way, Bubba," MayBelle said. "These boys have got them either a king snake or a coral, and they're doing their best to kill it."

"Well, I don't want to see it," said Avalene. "Let me get out on your side, Bubba. I don't want to get close to that thing."

Walking down the road toward the Big Caney graveyard, MayBelle brushed at her white collar with a kleenex Avalene had pulled out of a straw purse big enough to hold a water-melon. Although her niece had told her that the clay dust was all gone, MayBelle still felt like traces of red were down each seam of her dress and were working their way into the material of her underwear so that if she were to take all her clothes off there would be the outline of everything she had worn still visible on her. She kept flicking at her bodice until the tissue paper began shredding.

"Aunt MayBelle, stop that," said Avalene. "You're just getting little pieces of paper all over your dress. It looks worse than when you started."

Behind them Bubba was telling Sully just to sit in the shade on his lawn chair until B.J. came to get him and the dogs, and the two Dallas Cowboys were by now pounding the snake's head with a piece of lightwood pine. MayBelle could hear the steady sound all the way down the road to the graveyard, and it didn't fade out completely until she and Avalene had turned in at the gate opening through the hogwire fence around Big Caney.

Two Augusts ago the collection to pay for enclosing the grounds had reached a level high enough to begin construction, and old man Mape Willis had hired a crew of Indians from the reservation to dig the post holes and string the wire. The gang of Alabamas and Coushattas had done a good job, for the most part, with one exception. They had turned the angle irons for the barbed wire at the top of the fence in the wrong direction so that it looked like now the fence was designed to keep people and animals in rather than out.

Nobody ever broke out of a graveyard, though, thought MayBelle as she touched a hand to one of the barbs hard enough to feel a little pain, nor broke into one neither.

"Lookee here, lookee here," said Ned Felder, coming up to her in a toddling run, "MayBelle Holt and that smart little girl of Myrtle's. Let me hug y'all."

He did. Close enough and long enough to where MayBelle could see down into his left ear fringed with long gray bristles that he kept mashing into the side of her face.

"My," she said, "Ned, goodness sakes. Give me a breath."

All across the expanse of yard in front of the old church building, people were coming together in little clots and bunches, pulling and grabbing at each other as if they were afraid of falling if they weren't able to get hold of an arm or a shoulder or a neck. It looks like at the beginning of a wrestling match on television, she thought. When the two of them first reach out to touch each other's hands and arms before all the hitting and kicking and kneeing starts.

Right yonder Jim Swaylor is fixing to get a hammerlock on that youngest Popp girl, but she's trying to turn it into a come-along hold. And the Murphy cousins are a tag-team working on just the one person, Maggie Lee Floyd, holding onto her arms and about to run her into a turnbuckle.

Stepping carefully among the individual matches going on and away from Avalene who was stalled talking to one of the Overstreet girls, MayBelle moved across the yard up to the steps of the church building. The first steps she remembered seeing there had been made from a section from an oak tree, split in half and then smoothed with an axe. But that was when she still lived in Papa's house, and the oak steps had long ago rotted away and been replaced by a set of cast concrete ones donated by a Leggett contractor subject to fits of conscience at the end of drinking bouts. He had also given the Big Caney church an attic fan in 1957, but there was no attic for it in the building and no congregation there by then either.

MayBelle could see one of its blades as she leaned forward on the step to peer through the crack between the doors. Somebody had nailed stout boards across both some summer back to keep mischievous boys out. That hadn't worked on the boys, but it had on the older folks, so as she put an eye to the crack and smelled the hot dusty air inside the building MayBelle tried to remember the last time she had been inside.

It must have been a funeral because no regular services had been held there for over thirty years by now. She had sat just beside the aisle between the two sets of benches back near the front door, and she could close her eyes now and see the open coffin on the sawhorses in front of the pulpit. But when she tried to focus on the face, she couldn't pick out any features. Not hair if it was a woman, nor the part of the skull above the browline if it was a man. Whose nose was it, she wondered. The nose always sticks up in a coffin when they're dead and lying on their backs like that. Sometimes you can see just the tip of the nose over the edge of the casket from where you're sitting on one of the benches.

But it's never the right color or the right angle to tell who it is. You're not used to seeing somebody's nose from that angle, and it always looks like the flesh is sagging away from the point of it anyway. Papa's nose was never real sharp like it looked when he was dead on his back in that gray casket. And it didn't have those little sunk-in marks on the side of it either. That's why I thought it wasn't really him they had in there, and maybe that's why I didn't cry during the funeral. Everybody saw Myrtle carrying on and pulling at her hair and making all that racket and the tears just pouring all through her powder and rouge and off the point of her chin onto her dress front.

Old Man Stutts said something afterwards standing outside the building about how you could always tell who really loved their daddy at a funeral.

And he cut his eyes at me and hugged her, but I didn't show anything on my face then or later. Down by the spring I tried to cry while they were all up here hugging each other in the middle of the afternoon. But even then it didn't work no matter how much I opened my mouth and how hard I closed my eyes. I just looked at the water bubbling up in that spring in the wooden box he had built around it, and I didn't feel any tears in me at all. The water just kept on looking alive there, coming up and up in that cypress box and tasting just as cold to drink as ever when I knelt down to put my mouth in it. The only thing that was different was that I didn't care that time whether I got my elbows muddy or my dress wet. And I kept on drinking that spring water until my teeth hurt and my stomach wouldn't hold any more, but I was just as thirsty when they finally came and made me get in the car as when I had started drinking it.

"Aunt MayBelle," said somebody behind her, putting a hand on her right shoulder. "What are you trying to see in that old building? I bet you're remembering happy times in Sunday school, aren't you?"

It was B.J. wearing dark blue suit pants and a white short-sleeved shirt. He was carrying the coat to the suit slung over his left shoulder, and he looked hot enough to faint.

"Come see Mama," he said. "She's got something wrong and wants you to help her."

"Oh, Lord, B.J. Has she already started?"

"She's here, isn't she? That always means she's started. Please help me out on this, now. I got enough to worry about with my sermon coming up and meeting Brother Purkett and getting the Christian guard dogs organized."

B.J. was blinking his eyes behind his glasses at the rate of about once a heartbeat, and MayBelle knew exactly by that just how worked up his nerves were. If the speed of his blink reached the next level, he would begin to talk very rapidly about anything that came into his head, and if it reached the top rate, too fast to count the blinks accurately, in just a few minutes he'd begin panting like a dog in August, walking in tight circles, and somebody would have to hold him down.

"All right, honey," she said. "Go sit in your car and look at your sermon. I'll tend to your mama. Old Sully has got the dogs all calmed down."

"Nobody seems to understand that I don't want the dogs calmed down," B.J. said in a tight voice, but caught himself in time and spun around to walk off toward the fence.

He doesn't act any different from the time I opened the door on him and Barney Lee and that little girl from the quarter, MayBelle thought. That little thing had the blackest nipples, just as black and big as the pupils of those boys' eyes when they looked up at me standing in that door.

Myrtle was across the yard next to a stack of rakes and hoes, and she was using a long-bladed shovel to prop herself up against the fender of somebody's car, both hands clutching the handle hard enough to make her knuckles white. Bridget Warner was beside her, looking as if she wanted to be somewhere else.

"Here she is," Bridget shouted toward Myrtle's left ear, "here comes Miss MayBelle Holt. She'll know what you want."

"Yeah, but will I let her have it?" MayBelle said to Bridget.

"What? What?" said Myrtle in the tone of somebody saying a word from a foreign language. "What?"

"Oh, Miss MayBelle," Bridget said in a relieved voice, "your sister needs you to help her find some gravestones, I believe." She gestured to the right toward the stand of cedars and statuary, sharp and white in the light of noon. MayBelle looked away from the woman toward the groups of people beginning to work their way over to the graveyard gate in ones and twos.

"I'll take her over there, Bridget," she said. "Directly."

"Well, where is Avalene?" asked Bridget, a woman with a long body and legs too short for it. "I'm just dying to see her again this year."

"She's here. You won't be able to miss her." The struggle between Avalene Shackleford and Bridget Warner for the valedictorianship of the 1957 Class of Annette High School had been savage, fought on a day by day basis in each class taken for four long years. It had exhausted both women by its intensity, people later agreed, explaining the reason for the fact that neither one had done a full college course after finishing those years of high school effort. Oh, both had gone on to something. Avalene did the Drews Business College two year course and Bridget put in just over three semesters at Lamar Tech. But the field of contest had shifted, and the old opponent gone. Burton Shackleford said it was like when the war between Carmen Basilio and Sugar Ray Robinson ended.

"Just tell me," he demanded. "Who's going to give either one of them girls that edge now?"

Avalene up against Bridget was a test between a brute ability to memorize almost anything put before somebody and the trick of being able to do stated problems in algebra homework and exams. If allowed to look at a collection of words or maps or columns of facts long enough and if allowed to practice by copying things over and over frequently enough, Avalene could reproduce what she had swallowed and worried down almost just like it appeared in the beginning. Watching her do it was about like watching somebody vomit up something they had not chewed enough and had crammed down too fast.

Avalene would hump up over her desk full of paper and twist her upper body in movements so convulsive and dire that her teachers were often afraid during exams that she was literally going to begin to spit printed words and diagrams out of her mouth onto the surface in front of her.

"It's like it don't want to come up, but she's making it," Mr. Kettler, her world history teacher, once remarked in awe.

Bridget Warner, in contrast, had what Myrtle considered a low cunning, an intelligence akin to that of the monkeys in Herman Zoo in Houston which could play accordions and xylophones when you gave them little pieces of pinched-off banana. Mathematical problems and chemical and physical situations yielded themselves to Bridget with about no effort on her part.

"It comes to her just like turning on a faucet," Avalene would complain bitterly during the late night sessions with MayBelle and Myrtle. "She just sits down and writes out the answers like it's not even hurting her to do it." Avalene would then weep pitifully for a minute or two, and demand another rote question be put to her by one of the women for her memorized answer.

The combat ended the way it should have, both seniors tied for the highest average in the class and forced to compete head to head for supremacy. It was Mr. Strickland, principal of Annette High School, who came up with the idea of having a panel of teachers give the two girls an oral test over what they learned for the last four years.

"Then the one who gets the most answers right," he had explained in excitement to Elwood Kettler, "will be the winner, see, and the valedictorian, and the other will be the salutatorian."

"One gets the gold medal," said Mr. Kettler, well up on distinctions, "the other gets the silver. It's kind of a playoff."

When Avalene walked into Mr. Strickland's office that morning, she saw facing her across two folding tables placed end to end her senior English teacher, Mrs. Hooks, the shop and algebra teacher, Mr. Peebles, and Mr. Kettler himself, master of world history and offensive line play. Avalene was fresh from a long prayer on the floor of her mother's bedroom by her mother's side, and she had had a good breakfast of oatmeal and three biscuits. She was ready and had on her game face.

"The best thing about it," she later told people, "is that they couldn't make you work algebra and geometry problems in an oral test."

The only math questions she had, in fact, were those she knocked out of the park: who invented geometry? Where did he live? What did he write all his theorems on? A blackboard or the beach? And when Mrs. Hooks asked her to recite her favorite lines of poetry, Avalene knew she had it won. "The curfew tolls the knell of parting day," she began in a triumphant voice, and simply blew Bridget Warner off the map.

It was, as she later learned from something she read in a magazine in a doctor's waiting room, the peak experience of her life. Nothing ever touched it in intensity and meaning after that, not even those Friday afternoon sessions on the cot in the backroom of Mr. Boyd Purvis's business establishment. The sharp descent from that peak had left her bitter and wandering, and it was hard ever after to keep it out of her mind even when she was doing something supposed to be happy.

"Take me over there to the graveyard, MayBelle," said Myrtle, pushing off with her shovel from her lean against the fender of the car. "I feel like I'm as up to it as I'm going to get."

"Stay there for a few more minutes. I got to go scout it out. You know we never can remember which grave is Mama's and which Avis's."

"They haven't moved nothing in there, have they?" Myrtle asked in a quaver. "Since last year?"

"They don't move nothing in a graveyard, sister. They just put in new graves, and it makes it look like they moved the other ones. Let me go see."

Putting a hand up to her eyes to shade against the white glare off the sandy soil and the granite blocks of stone, MayBelle walked toward the open gate of the graveyard. She was careful to make a detour around Aunt Texas Alabama Nance who had positioned herself in a spot from which she could identify everybody who walked through the gap in the fence, but the old woman called out her name anyway.

"I'll talk to you after a while, Aunt Texas," she said. "I'm going to find Brother Bob's marker right now."

He was put in the third row of graves and to the left of the gate way down past Papa and almost to where the old magnolia stump used to be. It was harder to find him every year now since Ec Overstreet had pulled the old stump out with his tractor. The sand had crumbled into the depression left by the stump and had removed almost all traces of where it had been, so that was a sign nearly gone. But Bob's marker was easy to identify once you got close enough to it, a tree stump itself, cast in finished concrete and faithful in every detail of bark and knothole and axe mark.

Though he had died at only twenty-eight, MayBelle's oldest brother had already become a Woodman of the World and had earned the right of the stone reserved for the members of the organization. His name and lodge number were inscribed on a smooth place on the body of the stump, and an inscription about the brotherhood's relationship to the wilderness was cut in just below that.

As MayBelle walked past some members of the Murphy family, stopped in front of a headstone, she deliberately kept herself from looking in the direction of Papa's and Mama's graves, even though she could feel them pulling at the back and left side of her head. It was not time to let herself go to them yet, but this year, like all the others, they were impatient and wanted her to come to them first. Especially Papa, she thought, especially him, with his hands ready to put on each of my shoulders so he can look at me, and his mustache white and yellow at the edges, coming down so far you couldn't see any part of his upper lip.

Directly, she said to herself, directly I'll be there again. She shaded her eyes against the sunlight and looked down the row of headstones, counting from the one she was passing, the pink flat stone marking the place where one of the Nowlen girls was buried. It ought to be the seventh one from here, she knew, but something was changed since last year. She should be able to see the familiar stone tree trunk by looking through the top half of her glasses, but a new stone was in the way, a large whitish one reared up between her and Bob's marker.

When she got up to it, MayBelle walked around the front to read the inscription, a long one which started near the top and went almost all the way to the bottom. There was a color photograph on a round metal shield set somehow into the stone near the top of the monument. By leaning closer, MayBelle could see it pictured a muscular teenage youth dressed in a green and gold uniform of short pants and undershirt. He was crouched in a low squat and held a grapefruit-sized ball next to his head in his right hand. He appeared, from the intense expression on his face, to be listening to some message coming from deep inside the grayish ball, and he looked to be in a terrible strain as he tried to understand whatever it was saying to him.

135

Below the picture the words began: "Young man, you threw true. May we all do too." There were many more words running beneath that but MayBelle didn't finish reading them because just then someone tapped her on the shoulder.

"Miss Holt," said Algie Lee Bailey. "Howdy. Tommy was a shot putter. He put with the best of them."

MayBelle turned around to look at Algie Lee, a distant cousin with a head that looked like it belonged on a much taller man. He was the basketball coach of the Annette High School team and had once played the sport in college for two years.

"He was?" she said. "What finally killed him?"

"He was all-district," said Algie in a ruminant voice. "He'd have placed in state. Car wreck. He could forevermore put it."

"Young boys are bad to go too fast," MayBelle said to the coach.

"Yes ma'am. Went off that Shepherd bridge at a high rate of speed in a blue Dodge. Him and three others."

"Well," said MayBelle and turned back toward the row of stones, shining like glass in the glare.

"You have yourself a good time, Miss MayBelle," said Algie Lee and walked off sadly to look for other markers of young men, victims to the car crashes that infect the youth of Texas.

What did he put? MayBelle wondered for a moment as she turned toward Bob's concrete tree stump. I thought they throw or kick or hit all those balls.

When she reached her brother's grave, MayBelle put out a hand to touch a tree knot on one branch of the monument near the place where the dates were carved. Looking around to see that nobody else was near, she used the stone branch as support and leaned over to feel in an opening between the base and the monument itself. Years before, some rowdy boys had gone through Big Caney graveyard in the dead of night to see what damage they could inflict. They had succeeded in turning over several small gravestones and scrambling some others around among the graves, but the Woodmen of the World had built too eternally for them to be able to do more than turn Bob's marker slightly around on its foundation. So as MayBelle stooped toward the monument, she was able to slip her hand through an opening which extended a good two feet into the stone base.

At first she felt nothing but deep mulch, and a few twigs, but a deeper reach brought her hand to the ridged top of the bottle Van Ray Cox had put there the day before. It was more of the vodka she had had last, a new appearance of the Bear-King dancing on water, and it took her only a minute or two, crouching next to Bob's tree stump to pour the whole bottle into the large thermos she had stuck down in her big purse, the one Myrtle had not wanted her to bring to Big Caney because of its size and look.

"I know exactly what I'm doing," MayBelle had said to her early that morning standing barefoot in front of the bedroom mirror. "You pick your purse, sister, and I'll pick mine."

It's my cooler, she said to herself, my Sprite cooler, and it's going to do me good. She shook the thermos until it sloshed, rattling the whole tray of ice she had loaded it with that morning.

"Bob," she said out loud, "thank you kindly for holding that for me. You ain't got no use for it and besides, you always did keep more around than you could drink yourself."

MayBelle leaned closer to the tree trunk as though to listen for an answer, but after a minute she straightened up and poured herself a good measure from the thermos bottle into the cup that came with it. From way across the graveyard and two rows over, Jeanette Rae Collins watched MayBelle drink and remarked to her husband that it was sweet and kind of pitiful to see these old people wandering around talking to themselves in the middle of a cemetery.

"There's one of them," she said to Earl, "drinking some ice

137

water to keep from getting dehydrated. Isn't that Mrs. Myrtle Shackelford?"

Earl looked and said that it wasn't Myrtle but the other one and why didn't they get out of this sand bed and into the shade. His beige nylon shirt was sticking to his skin, and the sweat was making the patches of hair on his back show through.

Papa is buried between his two wives, Mama by his left hand and Avis by his right. His monument is the biggest one, and Mama's is the littlest even though she had more children by him than Avis did. Nine of our bunch to six by her, that top crop as Burton called them. You got to give them credit, though, for buying her that nice big stone with the angel and the lamb cut into it. They all gave money for it, and we couldn't get but five of us to put anything into buying one for Mama, and that was years after she was dead with nothing but a little piece of shiny metal to mark the foot of her grave.

MayBelle stepped back from the three long mounds of sand to see if she could find the identification tag put there by the county over fifty years ago. Either somebody had taken it for a souvenir or mean boys had sailed it off in the woods somewhere, for she couldn't see it even after poking in the lank grass and bitter weeds with the toe of her shoe. As she leaned over to see better, her heavy purse slipping off her shoulder and almost hitting the ground before she caught the strap just in time, MayBelle could feel Papa beginning to look at her.

His eyes on her made the left side of her face feel like it was drawing up, like it does when soap is on it and dries before you can rinse it off. Her face had been covered with it when the knock came at the door and it was so loud and fast she ran out of the bathroom to answer it without splashing water over her face. The whole time they were telling her that he was gone she kept thinking about the way her cheeks felt drying with the soap still on them. And all she wanted to do was go back to the bathroom and get her face clean while they tried to say he was dead without really saying he was dead.

She looked suddenly up at the stone, but he knew in time and there was nothing there but a name and some numbers. The sun caught some of the sparkle in the granite and took away the inscription, and she was looking at a thing that somebody had made with a machine and a chisel out of a piece of rock.

"Papa," she said, knowing better than what her eyes told her, "it's just Sprite and ice. But you don't know what that is, do you? It's soda water, like an old fashioned seven-up. You like it, it likes you."

Avis was dead and couldn't say or see or hear anything, but Mama could, no matter how much she made like she couldn't there beside him, her small gray stone with only her first name and the word wife beneath it.

"Mama can tell you. I wouldn't do anything like that, would I? Tell him, Mama."

But Mama looked off and held her breath as though she was hearing a bird singing far off and was trying to think what kind it was. It didn't interest her. Whatever it was was between MayBelle and Papa, and one of the other girls needed her more just then.

"I've got to go help Luella right now," MayBelle said. "With that dress I'm helping her make for her wedding. I promised her I would. You remember I told you that last Sunday out on the porch." She turned away from the stones toward another part of the graveyard, sand from the foot of Papa's mound gritting under her shoe soles.

"Not long," she said. "In just a little while. I'll be back here with you."

Luella was looking straight up toward the furthest fringe of dark needles at the top of the cedar next to her stone. The tree had been only head high when they put her there two days after her birthday, MayBelle remembered, and one of the men digging had cut some of the roots on one side with his shovel. I was worried about that tree, she thought. It looked like it would be crooked and not full on that one side, but here it's sixty years later, and the growing's all done, and you can't tell if you didn't already know that there's anything missing in the roots.

"Luella," she said out loud. "Good morning this hot day. Isn't the air just so still it's smothering?"

MayBelle leaned toward the headstone to read the inscription, slipping the large purse off her shoulder to rest on the ground. As she did, a trickle of sweat ran from her collar half-way down her chest and made her shiver. The stone was a whitish one that had darkened over the years with the elements, and the edges of the letters had blurred enough to make it seem they had always been part of the monument even when it had been lost in a mountain of stone underground.

Luella Ann Petry, ran the words of the first line of inscription, then the dates twenty-four years apart, and after that the words MayBelle had convinced Vance Petry to use instead of the Bible verse he and Luella's mother had wanted first.

"The first six words of John 3:16 will be right for Luella's markings," he had told MayBelle, reared up in that straight chair on the front porch of his house in the Holly Springs settlement. "If she had seen fit to live by them, she'd been here right now helping her mother in that kitchen instead of where she is yonder in Big Caney."

MayBelle didn't say what she thought, but instead looked directly into Vance's eyes until he had to look off over her shoulder into the deep stand of pines across the road.

"She lived by the Bible if anybody ever did, Mr. Petry. And she was taken, because it was too mean for her down here."

"She took herself," Vance Petry said and made a sound deep

in his throat that sounded like something inside was twisting another half-turn. "Took herself she did."

"She never," said a voice from just inside the screen door behind his straight chair. "She never. Luella died of a complete heart attack on her birthday."

"Yes, ma'am," said MayBelle to Luella's mother, a form outlined behind the dark screen. "It was that, all right. A complete heart attack and her just twenty-four."

Now sixty years later, in the hot middle of day MayBelle traced the letters with her fingers, gritty and warm beneath them in the sun. *Too Dear to Stay,* the words that had come to MayBelle in her sleep the same day it happened. Had it hurt much, she wondered that night after she heard, was the taste like swallowing oil or was it like fire all the way into every vein of her body.

When she first thought to ask Luella, years later at Big Caney after that time in Houston and her putting her own mark with the iron on the door facing of that room, Luella had smiled for the first time since she had been lying beneath her mound.

"It was sweet," she had whispered, "so sweet, like thin honey, and I couldn't drink it fast enough to satisfy me."

Two rows over, three or four members of some family MayBelle couldn't identify worked their way slowly from stone to stone, pointing at first one and the other before them. She looked away to watch the shade of the cedar creep a little closer to the base of Luella's monument.

"Lu Lu," MayBelle said to the headstone, "he's going to be here this time, I just know it. That second wife has died over in Conroe, I believe, and nobody's heard anything about Mattie Lou for years." The puff of wind worked at the edges of the cedar for a second, then gave up and died away without being able to move even one branch.

"I think Mattie must be living in a home out yonder in California somewhere," MayBelle said in a lower voice. "By herself."

At that Luella's eyes opened and flared for an instant before closing again there among the roots of the cedar, and after that she gave no more notice to the woman who had helped sew the dress, far away again in Holly Springs in the barn behind her father's house.

"You'll see. I promise you he'll show up this year, and I'll bring him out here to you."

She hears me, MayBelle thought, but she's afraid to hope it'll happen and that's why she's gone back deep again, quiet and still the way she was when her mama found her there in that half-finished dress with just the basting threads holding it together. It was hard to get it just right without her to try it on for me to see, but I worked on it all that night to finish. And I got through with the hemming just in time for them to put it on her, and I never hurried a stitch or had to tear out a thing I'd done neither. Everybody said it was the best I'd ever done, and they were right about that, even though they couldn't know how I had to do most of it by touch, afraid as I was to look at it except in little snatches when I just had to. All that lace around the bodice was the hardest part. That, and letting go of it when they came to take it away to put on her.

Bubba Shackleford turned from his spot by the gate into the graveyard and spoke to Avalene, who had one hand out to support Myrtle's elbow and the other burdened with five pounds of potato salad in the largest Tupperware container she owned.

"I believe that's her," he said, gesturing across the white blaze of tombstones and mounded graves. "Over yonder the other side of them people wearing straw hats."

"Where," said Myrtle in a tremulous voice coming from just

behind her gums.

"Where has she run off to? She was supposed to take me to Burton's grave."

"Just over yonder, Mama," said Avalene, trying to ease the potato salad to the ground without turning it over and at the same time pushing up on Myrtle's arm. "Look, can't you just lean up against that post for a minute and let me get rid of this Tupperware piece?"

"No, I can't, Little Sis. It's got resin coming out of it, and it'll get all over my sleeve and ruin it."

"Keep her balanced there for a minute," said Bubba, "and I'll get Aunt MayBelle's attention."

"Woo," he called, "woo, Aunt MayBelle."

"What is she drinking out of that Thermos?" Avalene asked. "That's the second cup since I've been watching her."

"Probably just ice water, Little Sis," Bubba said. "Ain't nothing lethal."

Myrtle stood moving her feet up and down as if preparing for the start of a sprint, each foot kicking up little puffs of white dust as she set it down again. "I feel a rumbling inside," she said.

"Be still, Mama. I'm going to lose this potato salad if you don't settle down." Avalene was beginning to feel the pressure of sweat building up beneath her pancake foundation and threatening to burst forth in large pink drops to fall all down the front of her dress. If Mr. Boyd Purvis showed up, she knew he couldn't stand to see her looking unfresh, and at the rate things were going she'd be sweated through all her hair and clothes before even the preaching started.

"Bubba," she said low between her teeth, "you go get MayBelle away from that graveyard and give me some relief."

"Hot, hot," said Myrtle, continuing her dusty march in place, "I want to go see Burton. I want to see him now."

The praying was about to start, and then the eating would begin. All morning long the weed pulling and grass cutting which had commenced at sun-up had gone on. The serious working of the graves was about finished, and most of the hoes and sickles and shovels were stacked against the inside edge of the fence by family and owner. Only a few of the Bannings were still chopping away at the bitterweeds, palmettoes and saw briars which had overgrown their plots since last year, and everybody knew that whole family was a slow and sorry bunch. So much so that this year Cyrus Banning had brought in a gasoline powered weed-eater to float over his mama's and daddy's graves, but people had complained so much about the lack of reverence engendered by the high-pitched squall of the machine that Butch Haywood had made him shut it off.

Later in the afternoon after everybody but that Moye bunch had finished eating dinner on the ground, the women at the graveyard working would tend to the final niceties of tidying up the ranks of graves and monuments. Old Lady Bartee would take her bucket of water and Spic and Span down to the foot of the burying ground where Lem's monument stood, and she would attack its surface with a steel brush and suds the way she had attacked the tobacco drippings around Lem's mouth with a wet dishrag when he was still alive on the side porch of their house. All across the rows of graves women dressed in their best clothes and their whitest shoes would kneel one more time to pluck out a clump of saw grass or rearrange a spray of plastic roses or steal some white gravel from the plots of the prosperous to supplement the pea gravel and flint stone lining the final beds of their departed.

Once at the Big Caney graveyard working a young woman from Rice University had showed up carrying two Japanese cameras and a German tape recorder and wearing a dress that looked like she had slept in it. She did folklore. She was particularly taken with the homage being paid the past lives of the widows with their husbands, she had said, and she was much gratified to be able to find that so many of them were willing to be interviewed.

"Tell me," she said to Maudie Dunlap, holding a silver microphone up to her mouth as though she were a dental hygienist trying to suck out excess secretions, "your feelings as you minister to the physical emblem of what's left of your time together with him. Is there an establishment of a closeness with him in this actual moment? Or do you view it as part of an ongoing process of relationship, a reaffirmation annually of a union begun those many years ago?" She looked encouragingly into Maudie's glasses, her own mouth slightly open as though to get Maudie started and her large black leatherette bag slung around behind her back to let her stand closer to the respondent.

"Am I on the air?" asked Maudie and poked a finger at the microphone.

"In a manner of speaking, yes."

"Well, what I think about when I tend Bill's grave is whether or not it looks as good as that Sharp boy's next to it. Now it does this year. But last year or maybe the one before they run some kind of a new cleaner in on me and got that stone next to Bill's looking real white and kind of slick like. That old Dutch Girl cleanser I was using just didn't cut it. But you know what I did?"

"No," said the feminist folklorist, backing up a step from Maudie. "No."

"What I did," said Maudie, reaching out to grasp the young woman's wrist so she could get the microphone close up enough to her mouth to satisfy her, "was to call up Eugene Pratt, my sister's boy in Houston. He works for NASA. And he brought me some of that cleaning chemical they use on them jet engines."

As the young woman walked off with her cameras and other equipment slapping at her back and sides in quick jerks, Maudie had called after her to say that the jet cleaner had worked better on Lem's stone than anything she had ever seen talked up either in the Coushatta County *Enterprise* or on the television set.

Old Man Fate Waldrup stood at the top of the concrete steps leading up to the nailed-shut church door, his straw Stetson in his left hand and his right lifted to his mouth to help him project better. His hair was clipped so close on the sides of his head that pink showed through, and it was so white on top that it had pale blue highlights in the sun. "Folks," he called in a long drawn out cry, "folks. Gather round, gather round."

Children all the way down at the spring in back of the hill on which the graveyard lay could hear him. Old women who had to listen to the television with their Japanese hearing aids turned all the way up spun around from the people they were talking to and looked toward the Big Caney church building. Bubba Shackleford stopped in the middle of a sentence, which was part of a long explanation he was delivering to Lon Anthony on why he ought to tear out the city sewage connection from his house on Washington street and go septic, to look at Old Man Waldrup.

Two of the Dobermans in the wire pen on the trailer behind Bubba's pickup fell away from a locked-jaw situation with one of the shepherds to sit back briefly on their haunches in a low growl. Sully, who had been alternately napping and switching the cattle prod off and on to watch the spark jump reared back so suddenly in the pickup bed that he bumped his head on the steel cab behind him. From their resting places by, in and on cars and trucks, from the furthermost row of graves, from the thickets surrounding the graveyard itself, from the bubbling boxed spring at the base of the hill, from wherever they were in East Texas in earshot they all began to move slowly toward the steps of the church building and the sound of Fate Waldrup's voice.

As they came toward him, some on canes, crutches and walkers, a few here and there in wheelchairs being pushed, some stepping lively and some limping, some fearful and inward and some as brash and assured as white-faced yearling cattle, Fate slipped quietly off the top step to yield to the preachers, he himself sole possessor of the gift of his calling voice but modest nonetheless.

By the time most of the crowd had gathered in the area in front of the church building, two younger men had replaced Fate at the top of the steps, one the Reverend B.J. Shackleford and the other Brother Tim Purkett of Leggett. B.J. stood looking over the bunches of people gathering slowly to a joining in front of him, a closing together of old and young and men and women and boys and girls, and from his vantage point at the top of the steps he could recognize that it looked like something he had seen before. What it put him in mind of was a human heart he had once watched in an operation on color television. It had been beating in slow motion, and the camera had steadily slowed it down so much you could see it sucking in before it expanded to kick the blood on out in its way through all the veins and arteries. Right before it did its most important work, the very thing the Lord had made it for, the human heart drew up to its littlest size and looked its very puniest. I'm going to remember that thought, B.J. noted to himself. That sucker'll preach.

Now, however, he stood with a wide pleasant smile on his face watching all these Big Caney folks gathering in toward him, and his smile was there because it ought to be and also, he found himself feeling, because he wanted it to be there too. He smiled wider at the thought of himself smiling at these people so pleasantly. It was true, he had learned a long time ago, that a smile was the best weapon a man could have and that only a fool didn't train himself to be able to produce one when he needed it.

Once, years ago when he was still in seminary in Dallas, a gang of hoodlum Mexicans had surrounded him on a side street near the campus and had threatened to cut notches in his gringo ears. B.J. had flat smiled the little greasers into the ground, fixing upon them a grin so broad and white that they had all walked off together in less than a minute, looking back over their tattooed shoulders to call him ugly names and make evil promises.

"Brothers and sisters," he began, widening his eyes to let more of the whites of them be visible, "let us pray." He could feel the Purkett fellow beside him drop his head so quickly into a reverent bow that his shoe leather creaked. Worse than that, he realized in the middle of his calculated pause before the first words of his prayer proper, the fellow was continuing to sink in a delayed topple and was actually now kneeling beside B.J.'s left leg, close enough to brush against the pants leg of his blue summer suit and head dropped so far forward that B.J. could see the knob of a vertebrae popped up on the back of the fellow's neck.

Something was also strange about the way Purkett was breathing so heavily, taking in long draughts of air as though he'd been denied oxygen for three minutes and expelling them so forcefully that the whole upper part of his body shook with the expiration. He's some kind of a damned Campbellite or a Fourfold Overcomer, B.J. thought, settling himself into a more comfortable stance a little further away from the man kneeling beside him. He's liable to go into tongues any minute or maybe start howling like a moonstruck wolf. And I am not going to let him buffalo me into getting down on this narrow cement step where these folks can't even see me and where I can't even get a good purchase for proper voice projection. If he thinks this kind of an apostolic stunt is going to carry the day here at Big Caney, he's got a lot of unmet needs he's going to have to bear.

"Lord of Hosts," B.J. said in a resonant tone, being sure to sound the *t* before the *s*, aware that many untrained cornfield preachers made the word sound more like hose rather than another term for multitude, "we beseech Thee to be here now with us at our yearly gathering in Thy name."

"Be here, Jesus," said a country nasal voice at B.J's feet, drawing out the last syllables a beat too long and then chopping it off so quickly that an *uh* sound hung in the air like a black bird.

Oh, it's going to be like that, huh, B.J. thought grimly. Well, I'll see if I can't change rhythms on your country ass. I'll just bring down the register some.

The new phrase he delivered he cast in a tone little different from conversation, but with enough volume to reach all but the committed deaf in the back fringes of the crowd before him. The sentence ended with a noun, of course, B.J. knowing better than to lose emphasis early on in a prayer by letting a preposition end things up in a phrase sequence, and Purkett seized the noun and threw it forth at the crowd as an affirmation.

"Time," he uttered, managing to stretch the syllable into two and not failing to add his trademark *uh* as an embroidered end note. Quickly shifting tactics and speed, B.J. upped the rate of his delivery by several words a minute, hardly pausing at the ends of phrases and therefore losing part of his audience but accomplishing his intention of confusing Purkett's timing for fully three or four sentences of moderate to good length. Peering out from the corner of his left eye, he could see Purkett's head nodding uncertainly in the course of B.J.'s delivery until near the end of the second sentence, then beginning to settle into a regular, though a necessarily more rapid, weave and bob. He's about got it, now, B.J. thought, helpless to change rhythm instantly and knowing that the next strong word he uttered would be echoed in that low-class country trash tone of the kneeler beside him.

It came almost before he got the word out himself, picked up by Purkett whose pace now matched B.J.'s step for step as they raced toward the finish line.

"Mothers," said Purkett in a modified bellow, and then more as the man had the gall to use B.J.'s word as a springboard for his own invention, a kind of verbal redneck grace note, B.J. was later to term it in conversation with Barney Lee. "Mothers of men," said Purkett, filling up every bit of open air between the end of B.J.'s completed sentence and the beginning of his new one.

Someone in the audience murmured in admiration of the phrase and jostled his neighbor with an elbow the same way he would have done watching a successful Houston Oiler touchdown pass on a slow-motion replay.

B.J.'s face flushed with blood, and he could hear his heart beating in his ears as he stood, head bowed and eyes closed in the oven of midday August in East Texas, a redneck peckerwood about to go into a foaming fit next to his left leg.

"Amen," B.J. said and walked off at speed in the direction of the Alabama-Coushatta Indian Quartet poised to begin singing when the praying ending and the feeding began. He could hear Purkett scrambling to his feet at the top of the cement steps, but he pretended not to notice that the man was reaching for his shoulder a full two strides too late to touch it.

As Avalene came in a half run up to B.J. and a good number of the crowd began moving toward Purkett still at the top of the steps, posed with his head bowed, and his arms dangling as though in abject awe before the throne of God, the Indian quartet burst into the first line of *I'm a Millionaire*. The lead singer, old Charlie Hunts Bear's youngest boy, threw his head back and launched his high-pitched yodel above the other darker voices which were setting a muted background thunder for his tenor.

"I'm a millionaire," sang Bobby Hunts Bear, "Jesus is floating me through the air."

"B.J.," said Avalene, her eyes blazing up into her brother's face, "did you ever? I have never felt more like killing somebody in the middle of a prayer in my whole life. Him on his knees in those old polyester pants about three inches too short for him just a yelling that stuff while you were trying to talk to the Lord."

"I don't want to talk about it, Little Sis. It gags me." B.J. paused and looked toward the stand of pines where the long boards had been set up on sawhorses for the women to lay out the dinner. He could see two rows of different colored dresses, straw hats here and there, a scattering of white gloves and a whole collection of white, gray and blue hairdos nodding as the women worked with casserole pans, tupperware containers and plastic and paper tableware. As he watched, a little breeze came in a breath and pulled at all the fabric there assembled.

"I do tell you one thing, though," he said to the dead air just above Avalene's head, his eyes still fixed on the food arrangements, "this day is not over yet, and I expect that when you throw a ball against a wall hard, it comes back hard."

"You will take that sapsucker out, all right," Avalene said in a grimly prideful tone. "I have no doubt about that. Why, he ain't seen the inside of a schoolhouse since he was carrying his lunch in a lard bucket."

Brother and sister fell silent, the air becoming increasingly filled with the sound of the Alabama-Coushatta Indian Quartet's stalking of the tune of *I'm a Millionaire*. They had about caught up with it near the end of the last verse, and just as the song drew to a close, Bobby Hunts Bear nailed the final note right on the head and lifted it until it hung in the midday heat as though he had just put a tomahawk through it.

"I don't care what folks say," a voice offered at B.J.'s elbow,

"Them Indians are singing pups." Hunts Bear finally let his prey fall to earth, and B.J. looked to see who had spoken. It was Pick Simmons, and he was wearing his corporal's uniform again this year, at least the parts of it which still fit him.

"You down just to the combat boots and your coat, I see," said B.J. and offered his hand for Pick to shake.

"Yessir, Brother Shackleford, I am still wearing the uniform of our arm forces. See my good conduct medal? And my campaign ribbons?"

"Uh huh," said B.J. "Well, good seeing you again this year."

"Good conduct means you didn't do nothing to get put in the guardhouse for. I didn't do nothing like that all the way from that English Channel into Normandy."

Smiling and nodding, B.J. began to ease toward a clump of people to his right with Avalene adroitly inserting herself between her brother and the veteran.

"Brother Shackleford," Pick called out as B.J. moved away, "I been everywhere. I been to France." His voice was a bugle.

"He keeps that helmet all polished up. You got to give him that," Avalene said to B.J.'s back. "It looks good every grave-yard working."

Bobby Hunts Bear was announcing musically that He comes to the garden alone. While the dew is still on the roses, added the baritones and the bass.

Avalene was standing in line by the boards and sawhorses, a regular chinaware plate which she had brought from home in her hand because she couldn't bear to eat off paper, not even the plastic-coated kind, when she saw him. Instantly her upper lip began itching, sharp enough to cause her to rub the back of her hand across it for relief, but she was careful not to touch her lipstick or drop the fork she was holding.

She often had direct physical responses when she saw Boyd Purvis unexpectedly, whether at lunch in one or the other of the small restaurants and luncheon counters she frequented on the job in Goodrich or in the Super D in Annette on Saturday mornings or as now at some place she had no earthly reason to expect he would appear. She had never had much opportunity for physical intimacy with men in high school or all through Drews Business College, but after she had gone to work at the lumber company and fallen into the sweetness of her Friday afternoons in the utility room off the rear of the front office, Avalene had discovered that a great physical readiness was hers.

She had attempted to describe the way it felt on several occasions to Mr. Purvis, but he hadn't seemed to want to listen. Whenever she mentioned the nature of her sensations, she could feel him tighten up laying there on top of her between him and the cot, his hair all sweaty and messed up and poking down into his eyes as the afternoon sun came through the crack at the top of the window where the pulled-down shade didn't fit right. It starts all down in my feet, she had told him, and I can feel it burning like fire in my shoulders, and then little lights start flashing in my eyes like it was a skyrocket show on television. And I feel like I'm waiting for it to thunder. I just got to hear it thunder. I'm dying for thunder.

Boyd had said nothing, but instead had got up real fast and put on his clothes so quickly it looked like his pants had not had time to set and were binding him. And he was gone while she was still on the cot with her blouse and bra all pushed up around her neck, having to go off so fast, he always said, because of something he had to do with the children. Either to help get supper for them or do Little League for little Warren or take Pearl to the dance class.

Once when he had said he had to cook supper for the children and that was why he couldn't stay but twenty minutes in their little room, Avalene had decided not to hurry on back to Annette to eat with Mama but to stop instead at the Booming Burger for an order of onion rings and a coke, and he had been there in his Buick with both children and Mrs. Purvis, too. And they had all waved at her just so friendly there in the car by herself with her mouth full of fried batter, feeling exactly like a fool in one of the last fully carhopped drive-ins in East Texas. Well, that was cooking supper for the kids, in a way, he had said later when she asked him about it there in the little cot room with one window set real high up on the wall. In a way of speaking.

Avalene looked back down at a bowl full of macaroni salad just in front of her and pushed a spoon deep into the middle of it, burying the whole thing out of sight so that all she could see of it was about half of the handle. Whoever had made the dish for the dinner on the ground had put some kind of little red specks in it, pimento maybe or chopped-up pepper, not cherry pieces, certainly, she thought as she stirred around in the bowl and watched the little macaroni pieces heave up and down.

"Looks good, doesn't it?" said the lady next to her, somebody Avalene knew she ought to know but didn't.

"Uh huh," sang Avalene in a pleasant hum and put about half a spoonful on her china plate.

What I am feeling when he does all that to me, she said to herself in a loud voice inside her head that only she could hear, is an orgasm. I have read about feelings like that in lots of different magazines, and I know what they are. They are real, as real as these sliced tomatoes in front of me, and I really have felt them. I do feel them. Strong.

"Why, Avalene Shackleford, I hope you save some of that for other people," Boyd Purvis said next to her ear just as she was putting back a slice of ham that looked like the edge of a center cut that had been out in the open air and sun too long.

Little Warren was standing right next to her, in between her and Boyd and so jammed up against the edge of the makeshift table that it looked like his collarbone was bowed by the pressure.

"Ain't there no fried chicken, Daddy?" he said in Boyd's voice, only a little higher.

"Why, Mr. Purvis," said Avalene stepping back from the table and speaking past the thing that seemed to be rising up in her throat to choke her before she could finish her sentence. "I didn't know you come to Big Caney."

"Is this here Boyd Purvis from Goodrich?" asked the lady who liked macaroni salad. "From Goodrich yonder in the lumberyard? Odell's boy?"

"Yes, ma'am," said Boyd, "last time I looked. Ha ha."

"Y'all have a good lunch then," said the woman and moved off toward a specimen of squash casserole.

"Once in a long while," said Boyd to Avalene, "I do."

"Do what?"

"Come to Big Caney to the graveyard working."

"She likes ham. Don't she, Daddy?" observed little Warren, watching Avalene put the fourth piece on her dinnerware, this last one about half fat and rind.

"Uh huh," said Boyd. "Go down to the end there and get some of that coconut cake like you like so much."

"I don't like that no more," Warren said, but he wandered in that direction anyway.

"Did you come for the preaching this time? Or do you have people here I don't know about?" Avalene managed to say in a voice close to the one she used with walk-in customers in the lumber store. She watched her hand drive the fork through another piece of ham so hard it made a screeching sound on the platter. It had pictures of little bitty Englishmen wearing top hats all around the edge, she noted. They appeared to be jumping up into the air either in a dance or because they were so happy to have pork grease all over them.

155

"I come to Big Caney to see you," said Boyd Purvis, looking around sharply as he spoke, his plastic-coated plate still empty even though he had already come several feet down the sawhorse table.

A tingle started up deep inside Avalene's head, somewhere far behind her nose and almost in the middle of where it felt like her words were located when she was thinking about something hard to remember. The capitols of the New England states, maybe, or the order of the planets starting fartherest from the sun.

She opened her mouth to say something, but didn't, and was happy to see that her hand had decided there was enough ham on her plate. It had stopped spearing pieces of meat and was now pointing with the fork toward a spot on the table where there wasn't anything to eat at all.

"You," said Boyd. "To see you. I couldn't seem to get enough of you last Friday. So I says, hey, go to the graveyard working. She'll be there with her folks."

"Oh," Avalene said. "Your plate is still empty. Nothing to eat on it at all."

"We need to talk sometime. I feel like everything is getting so close on me I can't get my breath."

"You mean today? Here at Big Caney?"

"Well," said Boyd and reached finally for a spoonhandle. "I mean yeah. You know, a little bit."

"Down by the spring," Avalene heard herself say to the plate full of ham in her left hand. "During the preaching." Boyd nodded and walked past her toward the pole beans.

I won't be able to eat any of this meat, she thought. I probably won't even finish this little dab of macaroni salad.

Two of the Dobermans were lunging at Bubba's hand where

it rested on the edge of the trailer bed on the safe side of the hogwire. The animals were almost completely silent, only a low whimper escaping now and then from one of them as its head came so tantalizingly close to the piece of meat it wanted.

"You say it's Christian guard dogs?" asked a small dark man dressed in a suit three sizes too large for him, its cuffs rolled up two turns over white patent leather shoes.

"Incorporated," said Bubba. "That's the name of the company, see, Tump. It don't mean that the dogs is anything but dogs." He turned his head to look over his shoulder at the Doberman gnashing the hog wire. "Trained killers, I mean to tell you."

"What's B.J. got them here at the graveyard for?" Lon Anthony asked through a huge cloud of Bull Durham smoke surrounding his head. "Is he going to run him some hippies with them?"

The men standing around Bubba and the trailer load of dogs looked up from the various parts of the immediate landscape they had been studying to laugh and to see what effect Lon's words had had on the old Shackleford boy, the septic tank one.

"Naw," Bubba said. "Not to really run nothing, but just only to demonstrate them. Ain't that right, Uncle Sully?"

The old black man perched on the edge of the pickup bed cackled, said "yessuh, Mr. Bubba" several times and nodded so hard he almost toppled off his resting place.

"Show these gentlemen that cattle prod, Uncle Sully," commanded Bubba genially. "Hit that switch a time or two."

Hopping into the bed of the pickup adroitly, Sully rummaged around for a few seconds and came up with the silver and red metal cylinder in one hand and the Johnny Bench catcher's mask in the other. He donned the mask, pointed the end of the prod in the direction of the cage of dogs and clicked the switch on and off rapidly so that a thin spark of electricity jumped back and forth at the end of the instrument as though not decided whether to stay or go. The Dobermans lost interest in Bubba's unattainable hand and joined the German shepherds in a roil of movement at the end of the cage fartherest from Sully, tails dropped and teeth bared.

"They respect that thing," Bubba said proudly. "Them boosters have learned to admire the power of electrical charges." He looked fondly at the scene of man and animal before him and went on. "Can you imagine what these here dogs would do to somebody trying to bust in your house?"

"A nigger," said Walking Jones who had had nothing to utter before this point. "Trying to come in on you."

"Or a Mexican," added Tump Barlow.

"I praise God it ain't a Mexican or a picture show neither one within twenty miles of here," said Walking Jones, roused by the spectacle to comment further.

"Yeah," Fred Turner allowed, "but it is a hippie or two around here." He looked knowingly over at a group of younger men walking up to observe the black man with the electric baton and the trailer load of snapping dogs. Prominent in the new bunch were the twin sons of Mrs. Floydada Mayfield, longhairs who went to Sam Houston State University over in Huntsville and came home every weekend to tend the marijuana crop they had planted in among their mama's tomatoes and pole beans.

"Far out," opined Tim Mayfield, running his fingers first through his hair and then both sides of his mutton chop sideburns as he spoke.

"Oh, wow," seconded Jim Mayfield, as always about two beats behind the actions of his twin but nonetheless in tune. "Too much."

B.J. had left Bubba with strict instructions about the timing of the demonstration of Christian Guard Dogs, Incorporated: nothing formal was to be done with Sully and the dogs until after the eating and the preaching when everybody would be looking for entertainment, and nothing that could be viewed as sacrilegious by the Big Caney pilgrims could be allowed at all.

"These people are here not only for the fun of pulling the weeds off their folks's graves but for the reverence of it, too, Bubba," B.J. had said, "and we can't afford to do anything with the guard dog project that'll give them a chance to act offended and not think about buying into this thing."

But just look at everybody coming up to look at what's going on here with Sully and these dogs, Bubba said to himself. I just got to take advantage of this here interest somehow.

"Folks," he said, inspired, jumping up on the back bumper of the pickup and then into the truck bed itself, "folks, we are going to give y'all a real chance to see these Dobermans and shepherds in action later on in the day. But I would like to let you see just a little bit of the results of the training these fine animals have been going through." He spun around on one foot and pointed as he had once seen a magician do in a stage show back when the Texan Theatre was still open in Annette.

"Uncle Sully," said Bubba, "get that big one's attention."

As the little black man with the electric baton worked his way around the cage, his overcoat tightly buttoned and his arm extended, Bubba Shackleford looked over the crowd of men and boys gathering for the show. I wonder, he thought, if I could say a few words about how the septic system is got it all over the running sewage line after all of these folks has had a chance to see one of these dogs get an electrical shock.

Myrtle leaned against the fender of somebody's big green car, her left foot pushed against a small stub left the day before after Lonnie Boatright had run a brush hog over the stand of young pine saplings trying to establish themselves in the yard of the Big Caney chapel. The stub was an advantage to Myrtle because it let her keep one foot higher than the other, thus tilting the level of the green and yellow fluids in her body and allowing her a measure of control she didn't have when standing flatfooted on the ground. Still it was a struggle. The warring vapors generated by the two kinds of fluids mixed in her reluctantly, and she could feel a premonitory surge beginning somewhere deep within, down where she imagined her liver extended out to touch her right kidney and just the edge of the small cavity where her gall bladder had been.

That operation ten years ago had both relieved and damned, she always believed. The gall bladder had had to go, she often told MayBelle and Avalene and any other person who happened to walk through the living room between her and the Dumont TV. But when the doctors took it from her with all the bitterness it had sent foaming up into the back of her throat when she lay sleepless in her bed in the dark hours of midnight, they had left a gap in the geography of her interior, a vacancy where one should not be.

"It's not right," she would say in deep accusation and grief, "to leave a little hole the size of a coin purse in the right side of a lady's bowel cavity where all them stray fluids and gasses can seep and gather. It gives them a chance to react against one another."

Maybe, she thought as she worked her buttocks gradually along the fender of the green car, if I can force a bend in my stomach lining by pushing against that stub and leaning over I can get some relief. She shut her eyes, ground her teeth, and it came, sudden and sweet, and with only the slightest audible announcement in comparison to its duration and strength.

"Sweet savior," Myrtle said out loud, her face smoothed by gratitude and ease, "Thy precious will be done."

She straightened up and looked around her, alone against the heap of metal behind her ticking with heat in the August sun. MayBelle, of course, was nowhere to be seen, though she had distinctly told B.J. to fetch her to be an escort to Mama and Papa and Burton and the others. Looking past a bunch of Murphys, she could see Avalene at the table standing next to a short blonde boy in a baseball cap, and behind her, the growling and snapping of that load of dogs told her where her middle child was likely to be.

Not a soul paying a bit of attention to me, she thought, like always, and it's me financing the whole trip out here with that Sinclair gas I bought for that septic tank pickup. MayBelle is likely out there mooning over that Petry girl's headstone or sneaking a look at Burton's. I better not catch her doing it or saying anything against him. He never thought of her as nothing more than a nuisance and a case for pity right from the time she just moved in with us, lock stock and barrel. And me fixing to deliver, thinking I could get some help from her with the house and the baby after it came. Nothing came of that, naturally, and nothing resembling work from her has come since then, neither.

A tiny bubble announced itself shyly, but Myrtle refused to recognize it beyond exerting a little more pressure on the stub beneath her foot.

And that mess in Houston. Who was it did for her, then? Who piled in that old Star car of hers she thought more of than she did even of Papa and hauled her in the middle of the night so nobody would know she was gone all the way to Harris County?

"Who?" Myrtle said to the bubble, "Who was it?" Coaxed, it answered, and a timely utterance gave her thought relief.

The fluids, yellow and green, slid into a rough balance, and Myrtle was able to put both feet solidly on the earth, flat against the sandy soil of Big Caney burying ground. The foot she had used to push against the pine stub still tingled and throbbed, but overall her system seemed in better proportion than it had been all day, starting that morning when she had had to put up with

MayBelle's evil tongue all through breakfast and while she was struggling into the black dress with the open lace bodice and the fretwork around the neck.

MayBelle had made some remark that Myrtle had not been able to hear, pinioned as she was with the dress half on over her head and her unable to move or even get her breath for fear of ripping the seams. Myrtle knew it was something against her breasts, though, no matter how her sister kept saying, "I'm not hearing, I'm not listening" in kind of chant as Myrtle tried to get back at her.

She never could stand the fact that I was so busty and the way it made all of them look at them and want to touch. Every dance in them old Holly Springs home places they all wanted to dance with me and rub up against my chest. They always looked like they were dying the way they'd close their eyes and get a real sad look around their mouths when I'd breathe in and push them up against them. There wasn't any low cut dresses back then, so they couldn't see down inside my clothes, but that didn't stop them from fighting to get next to me. The first time I let Burton get his hand on one he breathed out so long a breath I thought he was about to faint. He didn't even know what to do with it. None of them ever did, but Lord they just had to have their hands all over them.

That's why I kept him. Even after he figured out about me and that roomer that time. Sharp was his name. Little, but he knew what to do. Burton couldn't give up my breasts even though there wasn't a thing he knew to do with them. He got so mad that time he cussed me and broke all the windows on one side of the house with his fists, and then he came crying back just to get them in his hand again. And saying all the time that he couldn't seem to get final satisfaction from them because there wasn't no real way he could ever have them.

That's what broke her that time when she ran up to our bedroom door like a crazy woman with that flat iron in her hand. I made him stop and lock that thumblatch, and she just pounded that door facing until it was marks and scars so deep in it that the biggest carpenter's plane wouldn't smooth them out. And her hollering that trash and lies about stuff happening in that car of hers. What it was that night was her drunk again and not having a man to love her up, and she couldn't stand to know we was at it in that bedroom. I never could keep quiet.

After the last time she hit that facing and the handle broke off the iron and she ran on off into the dark somewhere, he came on back to me in the bed there. He had a hard time being able to do anything else, but I wanted it so much then I just had to get him ready to come inside me again, and it was my breasts that did it for me. He couldn't keep nothing in his head when I lifted my nightgown up over them and made him look.

"Can I fix you a plate, Mrs. Shackleford?"

Birthalene Miller stood in front of Myrtle with a handful of plastic utensils and a faceful of Christian fellowship aimed toward the old lady whose three children were all there at the graveyard working but not a one seeing about her.

"Are you one of the Miller girls?" asked Myrtle, pushing off from the side of the green car to head toward the long row of feeding Baptists.

"Yes, honey, help me see if I can find something I can eat."

On the way to the table Birthalene said it was real hot, and Myrtle told her how she had suffered beneath the feather comforter the night before while she was hiding from lights flashing outside her house in a strange but regular pattern until dawn.

It had seemed like everything on the sawhorse table looked good, so MayBelle had filled up a plate until it was brimming, her first time through the line. Field peas, some squash casserole, a piece of fried chicken (dark meat), two little cornbread pieces baked in the shape of miniature ears of corn, a dab of what looked like eggplant, something else with too much salt in it. But when she had gone off to sit in a folding lawn chair in the shade of one of the big sweet gum trees she had found that she could swallow none of it, finally having to spit the first bite she had put in her mouth back into a paper napkin after she had chewed it for fully a minute. After she had drunk another half cup of the mixture from her thermos, though, and watched the shade creep away from overhead until she was half into the sun, she discovered herself wanting to eat something sweet, maybe a spoonful of cobbler or pudding. Hadn't she seen Old Lady Garner over there? If so, there was bound to be a blackberry cobbler worth eating somewhere on the table if Bubba hadn't already got to it. He and everybody else had.

On her way back to the lawnchair with a serving of banana pudding on her plate, she heard Myrtle call her name in a high voice which MayBelle knew her sister was causing to quaver for dramatic effect, but she refused to look over at the Shackleford family group just a few feet away, pretending instead that she didn't hear because of the racket from a bunch of young boys picking on guitars, and hitting a drum as they launched into an up-tempo hymn.

The one standing in front of the other three, a tall thin boy with flowing black hair and a reddish mustache, reminded her a little of the way somebody used to look, but she couldn't remember who it was until she had sat down again and put the first spoon of banana pudding in her mouth. From the sour taste of soda and the reluctance of the pudding to melt, she recognized its maker.

"Estelle Collins," she said aloud. "All she has ever cared about is the way something looks on the plate."

Off to the side the band hammered its way to the last note of the hymn and stopped, almost all of them at the same time.

When the lead singer had finished his last twang on the guitar he stepped up to the portable microphone in front of him and said some words about singing something a little different now, and as he did, it came to her. He was like her dead brother and him too the way his hair shone almost blueblack in the sun and the little tilt he had to his head when he opened his mouth to talk.

I'm getting as bad as Old Aunt Texas, she thought and set the banana pudding down beside her chair. Believing everybody I see is somebody I used to know. Next thing I'll be calling these longhaired boys Papa and asking for a nickel for some candy. Then they'll be sending me to Rusk instead of Myrtle.

By the time she had filled her thermos cup to within an inch of the top the lead singer had finished counting to four and the other three boys had joined him in announcing in a shout to all the folks at Big Caney that "You might think I'm delirious the way I run you down." The rest of the words MayBelle couldn't pick up among all the uproar from the guitars and the clashing cymbal that the drummer was hitting as though he were mad at it, so she concentrated instead on finishing her cup of vodka so as to be able to pour herself another one.

It's as clear as water and as cold as Big Caney spring. You can't hardly even taste it for the ice in it when it's going down. When it's clear and cold like this, spring water is nothing but temperature on your teeth. The only thing that tastes at all is whatever you dipped it out of the spring with. Maybe a gourd made into a dipper so there's a kind of a wood flavor to the water, or like the time he used the brim of his Stetson hat to scoop some for me to taste, and I could feel the edge of it against my lips like velvet tickling until I had to lick my lips to make it stop.

She let the cup tilt back and forth in her hand, watching the ice slide from one side to the other of the plastic container, now completely in the sun as the shade continued to draw steadily away from where she sat. The plate of banana pudding beside her showed no sign of melting yet, and the meringue on top glistened in the light like the paint on a new car.

You sticky mess, all you do is sit there and look good, like a brand new penny, but you taste just as sour as death, and I won't have any more of it, never again in this world. In a little while I'm going to get out of this sun and go back on down there again, through those huckleberry bushes and briars all the way to the bottom. And it'll be dark there by the water like it always is, and everything's that green will look almost black there in the cool where the spring's bubbling. He said that going into me was like going into the woods. It's dark and quiet and you're afraid something scary is going to happen, and it might get you.

"You the big man," Sully said to the closest Doberman, the one that had been growling so long and hard that slaver hung from its jaws like icicles. "You Mr. Muhammed Ali, I reckon."

He leaned over from where he was sitting on the truck tailgate and rattled the hogwire of the pen with his left hand. A surge of Dobermans and shepherds answered so quickly that Sully almost lost his balance drawing his hand back.

"Ooo wee," he said, sliding far enough along the edge of the truck bed to be able to pat the cattle prod with his right hand, "you boosters act like you ain't had no jellyroll for the longest time."

Two of the dogs in front, seeing Sully's destination, lurched back deep enough into the cage to cause the ones behind to snarl and snap at the hindquarters ahead. A boil of fangs, dropped tails and yelps rocked the cage from side to side until Sully reached through the wire with the electric prod and touched the side of a Doberman which had just earned a killing hold on a German shepherd's throat. The spark of electricity and the sound of the Doberman's howl broke up sufficiently for Sully to be able to sit back on the tailgate of the pickup and address himself to the guard dogs once again.

"I was just saying that you boys has got a shortage in the jellyroll department, and that's what's got you all nervous and high strung. Me, I gets my jellyroll regular ever time I needs it."

Sully paused to look directly into the mad eyes of the dog he'd just put the fire to.

"You see, Mr. Muhammed Ali, I got me a big old slice of that jellyroll last night before the moon dropped. And it were good, too. Hee hee."

Sully leaned forward to talk more confidentially to the stock and assets of Christian Guard Dogs, Inc.

"You see what's happening around here at this white folks graveyard working this morning? It's all kinds of people suffering from jellyroll shortages around here. And only just a few of them has got enough and there ain't none got too much."

He shook a forefinger at a German shepherd who had just sat back and yawned so widely that his jaws popped.

"You don't believe Sully, Mr. German dog? Let me explain it out for you then. Number one," said Sully and touched his left thumb with his right counting finger. "Old Lady Holt what got down in the bed of fire ants the other night and liked it, she studying jellyroll from a long time back. It old and just about done got too stale to stomach. But she still remembering how it was.

"Number two, the preacher man what thinks he owns you boys, he done run into a new bull come into the herd and he's got to whip him or head for the deep thicket one. Preacher man ain't used to these here white ladies cutting their eyes at nobody but him. And that new bull act like he from the country. He live behind the post office about four miles deep, and he just get down and low at them heifers."

A Doberman that had been circling the tight circumference of the wire cage like a feeding shark made a sudden snap at the barrier, and Sully drew his shoulders up in indignation at the sound.

"You laughing at me? Or do you wants to know about number three? That one there's the old lady, the one what tries to show off her old female parts through the front of her clothes. My main woman Cora done told me about her. She act like she scared something's gonna get her, but she really scared ain't nothing ever gonna get her no more. Not no man, not no boy, not even Jesus want to grapple with that."

Sully stopped talking to the dogs to look toward the two lines of white people working the table full of food across the road in the churchyard. He could see that most of them had already filled their plates once and had wandered off to sit in folding lawn chairs or on quilts spread on the ground, and that the bulk of the crowd now gouging at the serving bowls and dishes was second- and third-timers.

"It gonna be something to eat here in a minute, gentlemen," he said, his gaze still fixed on the feeding multitude. "Maybe some fried chicken's backs and a little peas and cornbread."

He shook his finger at the closest dog. "Chocolate cake. Pudding. Some lady bring it."

Across the road two boys who had been making their servings of squash casserole into round gray balls by rolling them between their palms, suddenly turned on each other in fury, flinging the balls with loud shouts. Interested, Sully watched the mothers of the two lurch up from plastic and metal chairs to deliver ringing slaps to their children's faces and temples.

"Them little hellions needs a shot of old 'lectric, don't they, gentlemen," he said. "Right on they little behind asses."

"Later in the day," he went on, "I spect old 'lectric gonna do his natural business to somebody or something. Don't y'all? But wait up a minute. I done forgot to tell you dogs about number four, Mr. Septic Tank Man. He got his burden same as you and me. He afraid ain't nobody wants to shit like he wants them to do no more. He scare they wants to shit in these running pipes nowadays 'stead of in his big plastic tank. It's been his living he claim they trying to take away from him. People don't want to do their outhouse business right no more. They wants they shit to get on out of here these days. Not collect in just one spot." Sully hummed deep in his throat a mournful blues note and held it until his voice cracked and carried the song an octave higher. "Hard times," he sang, "it's a natural septic hard time."

"Here, Uncle Sully," said Avalene, stepping across the ditch and holding out a plate of food toward the old man, "it's something for you to eat. Have you got a fork on you to use?"

"No, ma'am, pretty white lady," Sully said, "but that's all right. I find a way to eat it."

At least Purkett was going first, and B.J. had the closing act. The country jaybird had jumped at the chance to open with the first sermon, betraying his uneducated background and his ignorance of congregation psychology. One of the first and last things B.J. had learned in seminary was the strategic advantages a build-up and summary rebuttal coming at the end gave the man speaking last to a Christian audience. Of course, the first man up had the initial chance to get them fresh and ready, but that situation assumed a crowd that had not just eaten four pounds of meat and vegetables and pie apiece. At a graveyard working the folks would be stunned to near death by the load in their bellies for fully an hour afterwards, and they wouldn't be able to respond to anything short of a public crucifixion with any real interest.

I'm ready, he thought, easing a hand into the back of his pants to make sure his shirt was still tucked in. I'll send that young peckerwood to Georgia. By the time I'm through, he will cheerfully buy himself a one-way bus ticket any direction just so long as it's out of here.

At the sound of Fate Waldrup's first call for attention, B.J. shot his cuffs, lifted each foot to rub the toes of his shoes against the back side of his pants leg, smoothed his hair down and moved modestly to the back of the gathering crowd as Purkett stood waiting by the church steps ready to begin. People walking past him to get closer to the speaker took notice of B.J., of course, some merely nodding, several speaking his name softly, one or two older women reaching out to touch his hand as they shuffled by, and a few of the younger ones too shy to speak but eagerly making good eye contact.

B.J. checked each face as it passed him, expecting to see Avalene who was always good luck to him at critical times like this one, but never found her and wondered at the lack. It wasn't like her not to be hanging at his elbow or leaning up to say something in his ear, her face working with emotion and her breath blowing lipstick and spearmint smells like a gale as she talked. Little Sis could be a pain magnified, but she gave him approval and faith like nobody else, not even Peachie who more and more wouldn't venture out of air-conditioned places to hear him preach and who had begun to complain lately at even having to go to every service in his own home church. Maybe Mama had been right about his marrying a Methodist, even one as eager to convert to the Baptist faith as Peachie had been when they had first got so much into heavy petting back at the college.

Blast her, B.J. said under his breath, and then at the instant pang of conscience that kicked up just beneath his breastbone added, if it be Thy will.

No time for that now. Up on the top step of the frame church, Purkett was beginning his sermon, and he did it by suddenly screaming in a high wail something so twisted by anguish that half the crowd turned to their neighbors to ask what he'd just said.

"Said, 'Mama, Jesus, your son is ableeding,'" Walking Jones volunteered in B.J.'s left ear. B.J. acted like he hadn't noticed that Jones had spoken, hoping that by ignoring the old man he'd not have to hear him again, but it didn't work. Instead, Jones took B.J.'s lack of acknowledgement to mean that he needed to repeat everything Brother Purkett said in the rest of his sermon to the preacher beside him, and he began to carry out the chore with great relish and odors from his mouth that revealed all he'd eaten that day and the total lack of attention he'd given oral hygiene during his entire life of roaming the highways and dirt roads of East Texas.

The rest of Purkett's sermon followed its beginning like chills follow fever and paroxysm follows a death blow. The Big Caney crowd felt its effects in its bowels, liver and lights, shifting where it stood as though great waves of wind were pushing the seed pods atop a stand of pigweed in an open field. People stood braced as though expecting a blow, feet planted and their shoulders hunched up toward their ears. Some held their eyeglasses to their heads with one hand as though expecting them to fly off from the force of Purkett's delivery, while here and there in the crowd others jiggled desperately from side to side, pulling at the front of their pants or dresses as if needing to relieve their bladders.

Across the way from where B.J. stood with Walking Jones translating at top speed into his ear, a woman dressed in a blue flowered dress cinched with a red plastic belt suddenly dropped to a squatting position and tugged at her shoes. Finally getting them both off, she lay back full on the ground and flung the shoes, one at a time with a deliberate right-hand motion up into

171

the air and, at the release of the last one, burst into a shrill singsong of syllables never before heard on this earth.

By the time Purkett had wound down into a slump on the top step of the church and uttered his last pronouncement, repeated by Jones in a voice so exhausted and empty that it sounded in B.J.'s ear merely as a rasp, fully half the crowd had joined the woman in her recline, and most of the rest stood stiff and tottering, muscles flexed as though lightning-touched.

"Where's my family?" B.J. asked Walking Jones, staring down into the gray hole of the man's mouth as if he were trying to read its content for signs. "Do you see anybody? Mama? MayBelle?"

Jones shook his head and walked off, his task of translation done, looking for a shady place to sit down.

Trembling, B.J. stepped carefully around a mother and daughter lying directly in front of him, their eyes staring fixed into the empty blue sky above them, and approached the church steps. As he stuck out his hand for Purkett to shake, he began to say the words he had prepared himself to utter but was cut off in midsentence.

"Try," said Purkett, so wet with sweat that even the knot in his tie was damp, "following that, Mr. College Preacher."

"He forevermore preached, didn't he, Aunt MayBelle," said Bubba Shackleford from where he stood with Barney Lee in the shade of a sycamore. "He let them know how the cow eat the cabbage."

"Yes ma'am," added Barney Lee, his face shining as though he had just taken a drink of hundred-proof whiskey, "that Brother Purkett did something for me today."

He paused and did a little skip that stirred up a bushel-sized cloud of dust at his feet that slowly drifted up until it looked to

MayBelle like Barney Lee was sinking into something gauzy.

"And you know what?," asked Barney Lee. "When he said what he said about the dead eating the living and speaking through their mouths, I felt something happen in me. It was right down inside my stomach area just above where it's been burning and tightening up on me all these months. It was like a little faucet just turned on and let some old bad fluids out and then rinsed them away with good clean water."

"What was it?" said Bubba.

"Why, just look," Barney Lee said, pointing toward the front of his khaki pants, sodden and dripping and beginning to coat over with the dust kicked up by his skipping movements. "I'm not ashamed of it. I'm proud to show what happens to the body of a believer when the Lord removes the burden of the unpardonable sin from him."

"I haven't seen that," said Bubba Shackleford, backing up a step deeper into the sycamore shade and looking down. "I don't believe I'd have told that."

"Neither one of you boys," said MayBelle, "had better say a word of any of what you've been talking about to B.J." She looked hard at the face of each one of the men and fixed on that of Bubba finally. "You hear me now?"

"Aw, Aunt MayBelle, we won't," Bubba said. "I know what you mean. Besides, I got to go get them dogs ready while B.J.'s preaching."

Then, turning toward Barney Lee, "You don't have to come with me now. No, maybe you ought to go off and do something about yourself."

"I don't need to do nothing about myself no more, praise God," Barney Lee said. "It's all on Jesus again, and I can relax and magnify His glory. Hubba mubba, hubba mubba."

MayBelle looked back once over her shoulder after she started down the long slope toward the spring and saw Bubba walking toward the road at a brisk rate with Barney Lee behind, weaving peacefully from side to side and steadily and happily losing ground.

That poor fat thing will eat so much now they'll have to help him in and out of bed after his mind's got so relieved, she thought. Best thing about his unpardonable sins is that they did help keep some weight off.

MayBelle had to cross fifty yards of open ground between the last stand of trees in the Big Caney churchyard and the line of dense thicket starting at the top of the hill that dropped off to the spring. By the time she reached the dark shade of the sawvines, yaupon and pines she felt the heat enough to stop for another drink from her thermos, the still unmelted ice clattering into her cup along with the vodka. The line of shade blinded her, and she paused just after entering it to drink and get her bearing before starting the descent to the dark water bubbling in the spring box below. From behind her came the sound of B.J.'s voice lifting to hit a word and then trailing off as he worked away at what was left of the spiritual readiness of the Big Caney graveyard workers.

Here is where his hand first brushed up against mine, just next to where that stump is now. It was a big bluegum tree that both of us couldn't reach around and have our fingers meet when we did. Some boys had cut into the bark to let the sap come out for them to chew, and I didn't notice it until I had gotten it all over the front of that blue dress with the white collar which I could never wear for nice again after that. I tried to tear it up for dust rags, but couldn't make myself ever use them and they stayed in that old pillow case for years until B.J. and Barney Lee got into them that time to make tails for their kites.

I came up from milking late one afternoon in March and saw the pieces of that blue dress flying high up with those boys' kites and thought as soon as I saw them what to do. And they were glad to put more string to them after I had half-run down to Old Man Deed's store to buy it for them, but neither one of the boys wanted to let the end of their kite string go until I promised to buy them some other ones and make Barney Lee a blackberry cobbler too. When they did, the wind was so high it took both of them up until they were just black dots with little blue tails to them, and we watched them get higher until it was too dark to see anymore and then I closed my eyes for just a minute, and when I looked again it was all gone for good.

MayBelle set the thermos down beside a rotted pine stump, careful not to let it fall over, and took her glasses off. She wiped them with the hem of her dress and after a minute picked up the thermos again and went on, deeper into the greenish shade leading down to the spring. At about the time she began to hear water trickling across the gravel bed, she lifted her gaze to look at a patch of sky that was letting a shaft of sunlight through, and she saw it.

It was mounted on a huckleberry bush about head high, just to the right of the trail, and almost hidden by the trunk of a sweet gum tree. Whoever had done it had taken pains and spent time.

It was a rubber doll that must have been twenty years old, judging from the chalky white to which it had faded, and it was fastened to the green huckleberry trunk with rusted wire. The arms and legs had been detached and repositioned so that now thighs grew from the shoulders and arms and hands dangled from the pelvis. Jutting hugely from between the arms was a penis whittled from a piece of cedar with care and great attention to detail. Leaning closer, MayBelle could see that even the opening was there, so perfectly smoothed that not a knife mark was visible. As she watched, a breeze took the top of the huckleberry and moved it a little, enough to rock the doll on the trunk back and forth so that the eyes lazily opened and shut in the green shade.

"Peek a boo," MayBelle said and toasted the figure with a slow drink from her thermos cup, "sweet doll-baby, I see you."

Gerald Duff

The doll winked both eyes once more and then clamped them slowly shut as the breeze died. The shade grew deeper as a cloud moved across the sun and plugged the gap the treetops had left.

"Did somebody turn you all upside down and backwards?" MayBelle asked and held her breath to hear an answer.

"Did he leave you with your feet where your hands are supposed to be? Did he make you walk on your knuckles and pick up things with your toes?"

The doll said nothing and wouldn't open its eyes.

"Listen," said MayBelle. "Doesn't it hurt for it to be like that all the time? Don't you ever wish it wasn't there at all? Don't you get tired of waiting for it to happen?"

A puff of wind came, and the eyes opened and a voice said something so faint that MayBelle couldn't make it out even though she leaned to hear it.

"Say it again," she whispered. "Tell me what you have to say."

"I can't," said the voice, louder this time, a woman's from somewhere behind the nodding doll, somewhere deeper in the green wall enclosing the spring. "Oh, Jesus," it said, "I can't stand it. Please, yes, yes."

The eyes opened slowly again and fixed. Empty, blue, porcelain, lashless. MayBelle looked deep into the eyes, and the eyes looked flatly into her.

A voice inside MayBelle whispered and told her where to look, and she saw across the open space behind the huckleberry and above the boxed spring what was there for her now and always had been.

In the green light filtered through the trees the woman knelt, her face shoved forward and down into the mulch of the forest floor, her hair strung with sweat and leaves. Behind her the man gave himself to a task, a job which he labored to complete, one hand to support, one to lead. The woman groaned beneath.

Above MayBelle the clouds moved, the sun dimmed, the trees bowed to a rising breeze. The water of Big Caney spring bubbled in its wooden box, crept over the still and polished pebbles and drained its way toward Double Pen Creek.

V

Witness

I t looked like to me that she just opened her arms apart and hugged that first one up to her. I never seen nothing like it before, and I have walked all over this country down in here. From Batson to Livingston and from Jasper to Schwab City. Ask anybody about Walking Jones. Everybody knows me and knows I don't lie. Time that second one got there she was down, of course, and you couldn't tell from where I was standing under that old sycamore whether she reached for that one, too, or not. I will tell you one thing, though. She never made a peep during the whole thing. All I could hear was them dogs snapping and growling like they will when they got something down. It was them Dobermans got there first, then the otherns right behind. Only reason they didn't go for me's

181

because I was kind of in behind that old tree like I said.

What I had done, see, was I had walked off from Brother Shackleford's preaching. I eased on down toward that path on down to the spring not because I was thirsty but because it was kind of pitiful to watch him up there. After that first fellow had finished, there wasn't nothing left for B.J. People was just lying around on the ground, most of them sitting up all right by then, but it wasn't no chance for B.J. to get them to pay no attention to him. Oh, he was giving it all he got. He had done pulled his tie off and was just a jumping up and down there on that top step. But you could tell it wasn't his real style. And that Purkett was just standing up there, leaned up against the wall a watching but he wasn't doing no amening this time. He didn't have to try to draw no notice no more. He had done had that.

People was not talking to each other or being unreverent while B.J. was preaching. It hadn't come to that. But kids was beginning to sneak off from their folks and slip off into the woods and across the road. And them mamas and daddies was so wore out by what Purkett had done to them that they wasn't even noticing them kids leaving. That's what done it. It was some of them Murphy boys, I'm just as certain as salvation about it, that done it. It was that littlest one of Gerald Murphy's that was the actual one that did it. Warren Lew.

They had been hanging around that cage full of them killer dogs all afternoon poking at them with sticks. And I hear that Bubba Shackleford, old Septic Tank himself, had been a putting that cattle prod to them early on to make folks see how mean they was and how they was ready to tear somebody up if they ever got the chance to. That poor old nigger man couldn't control them things. I bet you that one of them Murphy boys got his attention off to one side. Offered him a strawberry soda water or something and that's when that Warren had the opportunity to slip up and knock that latch loose with a rock or a tire tool or something.

They just came a boiling out of there, them first two, and just took off for that back part of the churchyard like they knowed where they was going. Didn't even stop to snap at them Murphy boys on the way. And by the time Old Sully got down off that truck bed and come after them, hell, they was already even with me by that sycamore tree. The rest of them followed that first two, and Sully was trying to run after them, and he was tripping over the hem of that long overcoat he had on in this heat trying to holler, and call them back. But you couldn't have heard that old man fifty feet away much less if you was a pack of dogs just been shot full of electricity for the last three hours.

And, like I said, she had done reached the top of that hill there coming up from getting herself a little cool drink of water, I guess, or maybe, you know having to go back on down that trail into the woods for a little visit. I hadn't even seen her until I looked around from watching them dogs a pounding across the churchyard to see where they was headed and she was standing there with her arms opened up, like I said, and I swear she was smiling. Or anyway she had this look on her face like she was glad something was fixing to happen. You know how a person will look when they think somebody is coming through a door that they want to see.

When that first one hit she just kind of welcomed it on in to her and then, of course, she went on over backwards, and her eyeglasses just went up in the air like something had throwed them up there. I never will forget the way they was flashing in the sun and how it seemed like they just stayed up there in the air for the longest time like it was slow motion on the TV. It was a funny thing, like I couldn't know to begin to try to get on over there to her or get some help until I had waited for the sun to quit glinting off them glasses and for them to fall on down to the ground.

Me and that old Sully got there about the same time, but to tell you the truth I was kind of reluctant to jump on in among them dogs the way they was just a ripping and slashing. But that old man, you got to give him the credit, he didn't hold back a minute. Just sailed on in there with that overcoat flapping every direction, but he couldn't do much good, of course, and by the time Tolar and Barlow and them Stutts boys got to us it was done too late to do anything for her. He got all cut hisself, Sully did. Fact of the matter is, them two head dogs had done run on off into the woods by then, and soon as Milton Stutts swung that lawn chair the first time at them German shepherds they just run on after them other first ones without staying to snap or growl at anybody else.

The dogs is still down in there somewhere, back on in them baygalls and hammocks and canebrakes by now, I reckon. And them boosters is going to be hell to kill or even to catch sight of. Tell me how you are going to run them things? Are you going to use bluetick or redbone or black and tan hounds to trail them dogs? Will a dog hunt a dog even? People are arguing about that right now and will be by the time the next graveyard working gets here. I don't believe they's anybody, not even old Font Nowlen, can get them things out of them thickets. They already wild. They'll be killing does and fawns for years to come in here around Big Caney. And by the time next year rolls around, and folks are reading the inscription on that new gravestone for Miss MayBelle Holt, them dogs will have forgot they ever belonged to anything human.

I seen the stone when it was being cut on by that fellow at Annette Memorial. He's a Syrian or Italian or something like that. B.J. picked out the verse for it, and him and Avalene paid to get it done, I hear. Both of them loved that old lady like she was their own Mama. Speaking of which, Myrtle never was able to get over what happened to her baby sister at the graveyard working. Went plumb nutty after it. Talking about little men with lights on their heads trying to get her. That's why they had to get her put over in that home in Huntsville right after it happened.

Bubba Shackleford has moved into the house there on Sunflower Road and Avalene has quit her job at the lumber yard there in Goodrich and has moved her stuff in with Bubba and his family. What really happened with that deal is she had to leave, I understand. Boyd Purvis had to run her off, I hear, because she wasn't cutting the mustard down there. She was a dead loss to him.

Bubba has got the yard in that house and in every one of old Mrs. Shackleford's rent houses all tore up with a backhoe, putting in new septic tanks in every one of them. He's just as busy as a one-legged man in a butt-kicking contest, I reckon.

What that scripture says on Miss MayBelle's grave marker is real long for a stone, I believe. I bet old B.J. feels guilty is why he sprung the money to have so much stonecutting done by that Syrian. He's as tight as his old daddy was. Burton, the one that died, oh several years ago now. Myrtle's second. I wrote it down on a piece of paper to show folks back in Annette when they ask me about what happened with them dogs and Miss MayBelle Holt at the graveyard working at Big Caney. Here, look at it. Tell me what it means. See if you can. People have asked me, and I just always say it's a puzzle.

The light of the body is the eye. If therefore thine eye be single, thy whole body shall be full of light.